"You temptress..."

Lloyd's voice was rich with desire.
"You were enchanting tonight in
your red-and-gold harem outfit.
But this is how I've longed to see you."

Deftly he drew away her last bits of
clothing, and she lay before him in the
soft firelight. "How I've wanted you,
Stephanie," he breathed, as his eyes
moved over her body. "Ever since I first
saw you, belligerent as hell at the idea
of being my housemate."

"I was afraid, Lloyd," she whispered.
"I still am."

"No more words." He laid a finger lightly
over her lips. "No more soul-searching, no
promises, no commitments. Just tonight...."

Dear Reader,

We at Harlequin are extremely proud to introduce our new series, **HARLEQUIN TEMPTATION**. Romance publishing today is exciting, expanding and innovative. We have responded to the ever-changing demands of you, the reader, by creating this new, more sensuous series. Between the covers of each **HARLEQUIN TEMPTATION** you will find an irresistible story to stimulate your imagination and warm your heart.

Styles in romance change, and these highly sensuous stories may not be to every reader's taste. But Harlequin continues its commitment to satisfy all your romance-reading needs with books of the highest quality. Our sincerest wish is that **HARLEQUIN TEMPTATION** will bring you many hours of pleasurable reading.

THE EDITORS

U.S.
HARLEQUIN TEMPTATION
2504 WEST SOUTHERN AVE.
TEMPE, ARIZONA
85282

CAN.
HARLEQUIN TEMPTATION
P.O. BOX 2800
POSTAL STATION "A"
WILLOWDALE, ONTARIO
M2N 5T5

Mingled Hearts

VICKI LEWIS THOMPSON

Harlequin Books

TORONTO • NEW YORK • LONDON
AMSTERDAM • PARIS • SYDNEY • HAMBURG
STOCKHOLM • ATHENS • TOKYO • MILAN

To Larry, for believing I could do it,
and to Mary, for showing me how.

———————————◆————◆———————————

Published May 1984

ISBN 0-373-25109-2

Printed in Canada

1

"YOU'RE BACKING OUT on me!" Stephanie dropped the pile of books into the packing carton and scrambled to her feet. "You're sticking me with a double mortgage payment!"

"No, no I'm not," Valerie wailed. "Please listen, Steph. There's another prospect already. Marge lined her up this morning. You won't be stuck, I promise." Her dark eyes pleaded for understanding.

"You expect me to share this place with some stranger?" Stephanie's face paled under its smattering of freckles. "Val, how could you?"

"Don't you judge me, Stephanie Collier." Valerie's tone deepened. "How would you have reacted if Gary suddenly reappeared and wanted to marry you?"

"I'd tell him to go straight to hell." Twin flames of anger lit her blue eyes, transforming the softness implied by her short blond curls and delicate features.

"Would you?" Valerie challenged.

For a moment Stephanie glared up at her friend. Arguments are harder to win when you're short, she thought. "I don't know, Val," she sighed.

"Maybe you're right. Maybe I'd do just what you're doing, but it's such a shock, when we've planned this so carefully."

"I know. I'm sorry, Steph, but I think it can still work out. Marge said this person is very interested in buying into a mingle."

"She'd better be. Not everyone in California loves the idea of owning half of an apartment." She slid her hands into the back pockets of her cutoffs and surveyed the living room cluttered with cardboard boxes and crumpled newspaper. "Do you know *anything* about this person?"

"A little. Her last name is Barclay, but I didn't get the first name. Marge just referred to her as Dr. Barclay. I think she's a marine biologist at Scripps." Valerie wandered to the large sliding doors that opened on their fourth story balcony. "That should be a selling point, you know. The institute's right over there." She waved her hand toward the curved shoreline north of La Jolla Cove.

Stephanie joined her friend at the open door and drew in a deep breath of salty air. Her eyes moved over the half-moon beach and sculptured sandstone cliffs of the cove, then traveled down the line of surf to the buildings of Scripps Institute of Oceanography. Damn. Val's decision to marry Jim was ruining everything.

"Maybe we should forget the whole thing, Val. I can't see rushing into a contract with some woman I don't know."

"Oh, no! You've got to go through with this.

What about your clinic? What about all the talk about independence? This mingle is your ticket, remember?" Val studied her earnestly.

"Sure I do, but part of the appeal was living here with you. I know what you're like, and I figured we could put up with each other." She grinned at the tall brunette next to her. "We've already adjusted to each other's imperfections."

"Hey, you're a psychologist, for Pete's sake. Are you telling me you're not flexible enough to adapt to someone new?"

Stephanie took a moment to digest the question. "You really know how to get to me, don't you? All right, so I'll meet this Dr. Barclay. How do we accomplish that?"

"Uh... you can meet her this morning. I told Marge you'd be here unpacking, so they'll be over any minute."

"What?" Stephanie stared down in dismay at her sweat shirt with holes in the elbows, her ragged cutoffs and two newsprint-splotched knees. "Really, Val, this is too much. Can you call them, give me time to take a shower and change clothes?"

Valerie's auburn hair brushed her shoulders as she shook her head. "I don't think so. Marge planned to show Dr. Barclay a couple of other places before coming here. They're on the road now."

"Other places? It doesn't sound like Dr. Barclay is 'lined up' to buy this mingle at all!"

"Yes she is," Valerie said hastily. "You know

Marge. She believes in clinching the sale by showing the client a couple of real dogs, then ending
with the property she wants to sell."

"Just remember that nothing happens unless I
agree to it." Stephanie felt her control of her life
slipping a notch.

"Of course." Valerie returned her attention to
the turquoise sweep of water. "It can still go the
way you planned, Steph. Remember it's only for a
year or two, until the market's right for you to turn
a nice profit. With this view, you should be able to
put up with all sorts of nasty habits from Dr. Barclay."

"It is beautiful, isn't it?"

"Yes, and it can still be yours." Covertly she eyed
her friend. "Forgive me?"

Stephanie glanced up in surprise and read the
guilt in Valerie's face. "Sure I do," she said quickly,
hugging the taller woman.

"Thanks." The strain eased from Valerie's delicate face, but the sound of the doorbell brought a
new look of apprehension. "I guess they're here,"
she said in a low tone.

Stephanie swallowed nervously. "Might as well
get this thing over with," she tossed quietly over
her shoulder, heading for the door. Pushing the
sleeves of her sweat shirt higher on her arms to
hide the holes, she took a deep breath and opened
the door.

"Oh, you're not—" She looked into eyes the
color of ripe wheat and felt an illogical tremor of
recognition. Yet she knew she'd never met the man

whose broad shoulders filled the doorway. "Excuse me, I was expecting...." Her apology died on her lips as she glimpsed Marge bustling up behind the stranger. No. It wasn't possible. There was some mistake.

"Hi, Stephanie!" Marge's carefully painted lips held on to a smile, although her green eyes were watchful, wary. "Can we come in?"

With growing suspicion Stephanie stood aside and allowed the man to pass. The aroma of pine-scented after-shave wafted past her as he strode by and glanced quickly into the room, as if looking for someone. Seeing only Valerie standing in the middle of the box-strewn living room, he turned back to Stephanie, his mouth opening with a question.

Marge forestalled him with a rapid introduction. "Dr. Barclay, I'd like you to meet Dr. Collier."

Silence stretched between them like a taut rubber band.

"You're—" they began in unison, then stopped, staring at each other in disbelief.

Stephanie recovered first and spun to face Marge. "I'm not sure what you thought you were doing, Marge, but if this is Dr. Barclay we've got to find another buyer!"

"Don't worry," barked the man. "If this is Dr. Collier, I'm not interested."

"Okay, okay. Wait a minute." Marge held up manicured hands. "All right, I admit I practiced a slight deception."

"*Slight* deception?" The man raked a shock of dark hair from his forehead. "I'd call it a major misrepresentation. You said the other buyer was a professor of psychology at the University of California at San Diego. Naturally I assumed—"

"Naturally you assumed a professor would be a man," Stephanie finished, thrusting out her chin defiantly. "After all, women seldom have the drive to achieve that kind of position, do they?" Fists clenched, she glared into his tawny eyes.

"Hey, don't pin that kind of thing on me." He squared his shoulders defensively. "Marge suggested buying into this—mingle, do you call it?—with someone else. How could I expect that you'd be a woman?"

"And how could I expect you'd be a man?" Stephanie retorted, her small frame quivering with indignation.

Marge sighed. "And if either of you had known the truth, you would have rejected the idea without meeting each other. So I took a chance."

"You haven't gained anything, Marge," Stephanie said. "I still reject the idea."

"That goes for me, too." The man jammed his hands into the pockets of his corduroy sports coat and stared at the churning sea beyond the balcony.

"Won't you at least look at it, Lloyd?" Marge begged.

Lloyd. So that's his name. Stephanie's eyes slid past the wayward lock of dark hair, down the straight bridge of his nose, over the grim mouth and strong chin. The collar of a white dress shirt lay open against the tan sports coat, and a few dark hairs curled upward from the V above the shirt button.

Without warning Lloyd's head swiveled and his eyes met hers, catching her in the act of staring.

"Finished?" he said softly.

"It's been a long time since I've seen a male chauvinist up close," she snapped, flushing to the roots of her blond curls.

The set of his mouth didn't change, but the tawny eyes twinkled. Damn him, he was laughing at her!

Nervously Valerie cleared her throat. "As long as Lloyd's here, it seems a shame not to show him around, Marge. You could start with the room which would have been mine."

"For the life of me, I can't see any point to it, but okay." Lloyd shrugged, turning to Marge. "Ready to conduct the grand tour?"

The real-estate woman's natural optimism bubbled forth. "Of course! I know how you must feel, Lloyd, but wait until you see the view from the bedroom. As I told you in the office, there are two master suites, each with its own bath. Stephanie's taken the one on the right, and Valerie chose the one on the left...." Her voice trailed off as she walked into the left-hand bedroom. Lloyd followed, stoic tolerance in his bearing.

"Valerie, so help me, if you knew this before—" Stephanie whirled to face her friend.

"I didn't! I swear I thought it was a woman," Valerie protested.

"What now?" Stephanie crossed her arms. "Any bright suggestions?"

"Well, there *are* two bedrooms, and you both work, so you probably would hardly see him, and—"

"Are you saying what I think you are?" Stephanie's blue eyes widened.

"He is kind of cute, Steph."

"I don't care if he's more adorable than the Gerber baby. He's a man, and I'm not sharing this place with a man. Period."

"Worried about what Jeremy will think?" Valerie pursed her lips teasingly.

"Hah. Have you ever known Jeremy to be possessive and jealous?"

"No, but then you've never proposed to live with another man before. After all, good old Jeremy has been trying to get you into bed for more than a year."

"Valerie!"

"Well, it's true." Valerie's eyes swept admiringly over Stephanie's small but enticingly curved frame. "But he doesn't turn you on, does he?"

"No," Stephanie admitted. "Which is too bad, because he's the logical person to become my partner in the clinic, and I have a feeling he won't settle for a platonic relationship."

"Probably not. But he's not right for you, anyway, Steph. You need someone more...more...." Lloyd and Marge reentered the living room. "More like him," Valerie finished under her breath.

"And of course you get the same spectacular view of the cove from the living room, which also

opens on the balcony through these sliding doors,"
Marge explained, pushing the door aside and silently inviting Lloyd to step onto the balcony. As if
to get away from her constant chatter, he walked
through the opening and over to the wrought-iron
railing, leaning his large hands against it as he
scanned the expanse of sparkling water.

Marge tiptoed over to Stephanie. "He loves the
view. I can see it in his eyes," she whispered con-
spiratorially. "I think we've got him."

"Marge, you're incredible!" Stephanie returned
in a low urgent tone. "We? I seem to recall telling
you I want no part of all this. It's out of the question."

"I wouldn't be so quick to throw away your
chance to live here, if I were you," Marge warned.
"The market's tight, and I can't guarantee someone
else, much less a woman, will come along. Frankly,
I think your choice is to live here with Lloyd Barclay or not live here at all. I know you can't handle
the payments alone, even for a few months."

"That's true." Stephanie felt a sinking sensation
in the pit of her stomach, as if events were pro-
pelling her toward an inevitable conclusion. "But
Marge, adjusting to a strange woman instead of
Valerie was shock enough. I can't see myself sharing this mingle with a man!"

"Why not? It's done all the time. Don't you ever
watch television?" Marge asked.

"Not much. I don't even own a set."

"But you're a psychologist," Valerie added. "You
of all people should be able to work out the logis-
tics of this."

"You made that point once before, Valerie. But I don't think they covered mingle living in graduate school." In desperation Stephanie appealed to the woman who appeared to hold her fate in her hands. "Isn't there any other way, Marge?"

The real-estate agent shook her perfectly coiffed head. "Not that I can see."

"Oh, lordy," Stephanie breathed, glancing furtively at the broad-shouldered figure on the balcony. She reviewed her original plan; the idea that had looked so promising. She and Valerie would have lived in the mingle for a year or two, then put it on the market when property values rose. Her share of the equity plus any profit would have allowed her to set up a private counseling agency. It was such a good plan. Why shouldn't it still work?

Logically, it shouldn't matter that her housemate would be a man instead of a woman. The mingle was not a permanent housing choice, only a step along the road to her own independence. But something about the set of the man's shoulders as he leaned against the railing disturbed her. Except for Gary, she'd always been able to handle the men in her life, to keep them in safe compartments where they didn't interfere with her goals. Something told her Lloyd Barclay would defy that kind of control. As if sensing her scrutiny, he turned, his golden eyes trained directly on her. For a moment their eyes locked, then each looked away as Lloyd strode back into the room.

"It's hard to argue with that wonderful view. I

can even see Scripps from here, so I can't find fault
with the convenience...."

Stephanie saw a difference in his face. The resistance was still there, but a gleam of anticipation
struggled to shine through those fascinating eyes. He
was beginning to consider the deal! Unexpectedly
her heart hammered against her ribs, and her breath
caught as she watched him come to a decision.

"Okay, Marge, I like the place, but I still have
some grave misgivings about the living arrangement. And the decision isn't all up to me, is it?
What about Stephanie's objections? Suppose she
has a boyfriend who might not appreciate having
her live with another man?"

Stephanie gasped. That was really laying it out
for everyone to see! Her heart kicked into a higher
gear. "As a matter of fact, there is someone," she
babbled, deciding on the spur of the moment that
Jeremy might be good protection from her rampant
thoughts. "Jeremy and I are practically engaged."
Deliberately she avoided Valerie's amused glance.

"Wouldn't he have a fit about this?" Lloyd
looked at her closely.

Stephanie shivered. The conversation was becoming far too personal. "I don't know." How
many obstacles should she eliminate? "He's also
on the psychology faculty at U-Cal, and he's very
liberal. He might not mind." *He won't give a damn, if
the truth be known,* she amended to herself.

"Then he's a fool," Lloyd muttered.

"Pardon me?" Stephanie thought she heard him,
but she wanted to be sure. Crazily, the words

warmed a place in her heart that had been cold for a long, long time.

"Nothing." Slowly Lloyd's golden eyes evaluated her, traveling lazily from tousled head to grubby sneakers. "I think you and I need to go to lunch and talk this over."

"Lunch?" Stephanie echoed. "I can't go to lunch like this!"

"I wasn't planning on candlelight and wine," he commented dryly. "And besides, that's the perfect outfit for riding on the back of my motorcycle."

"Motorcycle?"

"Yes." A smile twitched the corners of his mouth, and she found herself liking the way his eyes twinkled when he was amused. "It's a Yamaha 750. You don't mind, do you?"

"Of course not." *Except I've never ridden on a motorcycle.* The admission would have sounded silly coming from a twenty-six-year-old woman, so she did not make it. She remembered how frightened her father had been that his only child might become a mangled highway statistic. He had forbidden her to ride on motorcycles as long as she lived under his roof, and after she moved out, the opportunity had never arisen. Until now.

"I think that's a terrific idea," chortled Marge, nearly beside herself with glee.

"You didn't ride over here on his motorcycle, did you Marge?" Stephanie had difficulty imagining Marge, in her silk dress and velveteen blazer, astride a motorcycle.

"No, heavens no," laughed Marge, her mood

improving by the minute. "I drove my car, but Lloyd insisted on bringing his own transportation. Independent man." She winked at Stephanie, who chose to ignore her. "Well," she said, beaming, clasping her hands in front of her, "I'll just mosey back to the office."

"And I have a date with Jim for lunch," Valerie added. "Something about picking out a ring." Excitement shone in her dark eyes, and Stephanie gave her arm a quick squeeze.

"I *am* glad for you, Val."

"I'm glad for me, too, especially if things are going to work out for you," she replied significantly.

"We'll see," Stephanie answered. "I'll get my key and we can go, Lloyd." She grabbed the ring from the kitchen counter, then stopped to pull a few dollars from her wallet and stuff them in her pocket before following the others out the door. Her mother had always warned her about carrying emergency money. For the first time in her life, she understood her mother's meaning.

"Keep in touch," called Marge from behind the wheel of her powder-blue Cadillac.

"I will," answered Stephanie with as much gaiety as she could muster. Forlornly she stood beside the polished ebony cycle, watching Marge follow Valerie's Camaro out of the parking lot. To think how eagerly she had awaited this day!

"You'll need this." Lloyd thrust a white helmet in her direction, and she noticed he had already strapped a similar one over his dark hair. Feeling like left tackle on the football team, Stephanie set-

tled the bulky helmet on her head and fumbled
with the chin strap.

"Here, let me help you." His air of exasperation
irritated her. She thought she was being a pretty
good sport, agreeing to ride on the back of this
monster machine in the first place.

"I can do it," she flared, wishing she did not
sound as if she were seven years old.

"I doubt it. You've got it all wrong." Strong
fingers grasped the strap and snapped it deftly
in place, and Stephanie's face tingled where his
knuckles had brushed her cheek.

"Let's go," he said abruptly, turning to mount
the black leather seat and leaving her to scramble
on behind him. Awkwardly she swung up her bare
leg and managed to straddle the shiny machine.
"Ever ridden one of these before?"

His question caught her off guard. "No. That is,
my father thought—"

"Then put your arms around my waist," he cut
in, dismissing her attempt to explain her inexperi-
ence. "Try to feel the direction of my shifting
weight and shift yours accordingly. It's a little like
dancing."

She hesitated.

"Come on, Stephanie. Hold on. I can assure you
I'm much more frightened of you than you are of
me."

Reluctantly she slid her arms around his waist,
trying to block out the sensual delight of solid
muscles flexing as he bent to turn the key, bringing
the cycle to life. She tensed when he flipped up the

kickstand and gunned the engine, but managed to lean in the proper direction as they veered out of the parking lot.

With increasing speed Lloyd navigated the winding streets of La Jolla, tearing up and down its steep hills, while Stephanie struggled to keep a respectable distance between his body and hers. Finally she abandoned all propriety and hung on for dear life, her body pressed fearfully against his strong back.

As the ride continued and she did not fall off, her anxiety decreased enough for her to savor the sensation of crisp fall air rushing past her as the late-November sun warmed her back. Slowly she relaxed, allowing herself to experience the view flashing past—pines arching overhead, the occasional deep pink of bougainvillea, walkways bordered with marigolds.

Although she sensed they were moving away from the ocean, she could still smell the pungent sea air. Instinctively she moved with Lloyd, leaning easily with each curve mastered by the cycle's spinning wheels. Her awareness of Lloyd's body grew subtly, following in the wake of her fear. Gradually her palms registered the flat muscles stretched across his rib cage; her arms recorded the slim taper of his torso.

With each turn, her breasts became more sensitive to the shifting muscles of his back and her thighs tingled where they brushed his. *This ride had better end soon*, she prayed as her heartbeat increased. She wondered if Lloyd felt its thumping through his coat. *Maybe he'll just think I'm afraid.*

At last they swerved into the parking lot of a fast-food restaurant, and she sighed softly in relief, dropping her arms and pushing back on the seat. She glanced around in surprise, expecting a view of the ocean. Instead she saw an ordinary commercial corner, with the most immediate vista that of a self-service gas station.

"That's right." He grinned down at her as she climbed unsteadily from the back of the cycle. "No atmosphere. No ocean view. That's the way I wanted it. Let's see how we feel about this proposed arrangement when the glittering waves aren't seducing us into something which may be a terrible mistake, okay?"

Seducing. How she wished he had not used that word. The motorcycle ride had left her weak kneed and vulnerable.

"I guess you're right, Lloyd." *Keep it light, Stephanie.* "Besides, I was hungry for a cheeseburger and a chocolate shake, anyway." She managed to unsnap the strap of her helmet without his help and placed the headgear next to his on the back of the cycle.

"Me, too." His even teeth flashed again, and she noted with amazement that he seemed to be enjoying himself. The anger exhibited in the apartment was gone, replaced with a boyish warmth she found charming. Charming? Gary had once charmed her, too. She would have to be careful. All the signs were there, and they signaled danger. She could not risk another heartbreak. Not when all her plans were at stake.

"Is that a perm or the real thing?" His eyes roved appraisingly over her short blond curls.

"The frizz is real, I'm afraid. When I was little I hated it, but lately curly hair is in fashion, so I stopped using straighteners and 'came out of the closet,' so to speak."

"It suits you." He turned and headed for the chrome-and-glass doors of the restaurant before Stephanie could react to his unexpected compliment. *Careful, Stephanie,* she reminded herself. *Don't analyze his statements, looking for evidence that he's attracted to you. You don't want attraction. You want equity in this property so you can finance your own clinic. Get something going with Lloyd and the whole thing could be mucked up.* She followed him into the restaurant, massaging a tiny frown line from her forehead.

Within minutes they sat facing each other over a Formica-topped table, munching two dry cheeseburgers and sipping milkshakes from paper cups.

"You know, I was surprised you let me buy your lunch." Lloyd dipped a French fry into a pool of catsup on his hamburger wrapper. "Don't liberated women insist on paying their own way, especially in dealing with male-chauvinist types?"

Stephanie laid down her half-eaten cheeseburger and studied him for a minute. "I'll pay you back," she said in a low tone.

"Whoops! I stepped on your toes again. Sorry. I was just trying to get a handle on how fanatic you are."

"I'm a card-carrying member of the National Organization for Women, but I don't believe in burning bras. Is that what you mean?" she asked sweetly, digging in her pocket. "Here's my share of the tab." She slapped three dollar bills on the table.

"Whoa, Stephanie." His hand covered hers before she could jerk it back. "I invited you to lunch, such as it is, and I'll pay for it."

Alarm signals flashed in Stephanie's brain as the gentle but firm pressure of his hand sent the blood singing up her arm. Yes, indeed, she *was* attracted to him.

Slowly he turned her hand palm up and laid the bills in it. "Please take this back, and I'll try to watch my smart remarks." He pressed her fingers closed.

"Okay." She forced a lightness she did not feel into her voice. "Next time it'll be on me." *Next time*? What was she saying?

"Fine." His golden eyes held hers as if she were a fawn caught in the headlights of a hunter's truck. "What got you into this mingle business, Stephanie?"

"Money," she said simply. "I couldn't see any way on my salary to save enough to open my own psych clinic. This mingle is an investment. I plan to sell in a year or two and make enough profit to get me through the first six months of running my own business."

"But why a mingle? Why not a condo just for yourself?"

"That was Valerie's idea. She decided I ought to enjoy myself at the same time I built up equity. This setup is much nicer than anything I could have bought alone, and we were roommates in college, so we figured we could get along with each other."

"Why the big push to open your own clinic? Don't you enjoy teaching?"

"It's not bad." Slowly she stirred her milkshake with her straw before taking a sip of the creamy liquid. "But I got into psychology to help people with problems, not teach others to do that. I've always thought of teaching as a way to make money until I could open a clinic, but at the rate I'm being paid, it will take ten years before I can do it."

"Impatient, are you?" His golden eyes twinkled at her.

"Perhaps." She watched his even white teeth bite into the cheeseburger, and cursed herself for watching. "What about you, Lloyd?" His name felt strangely exhilarating on her lips. "If you'll pardon my saying so, a single man in your position should be able to afford a place all to himself."

"That's true. However, I made the mistake of getting married several years ago, and I'm still paying for it, literally." Bitterness invaded the golden warmth of his eyes.

"Still, you wouldn't have to buy into a mingle," she persisted. "You could get something cheaper and not have to share."

"True again." Some of the hostility faded from his face. "But Marge knows my weakness for waterfront property. And of course I thought the other buyer was a man."

Stephanie nodded. "And I assumed you were a woman. Marge did a number on both of us."

"Yep." He picked up another French fry. "How come your friend is backing out, by the way? Did she suddenly remember you snore?" His grin was disarming, and she chuckled.

"No, I have Cupid to thank for this mess. A former love returned and proposed."

"And left you holding the bag, or the mortgage in this case."

"Yes." It sounded disloyal, and she hurried to clear Valerie's name. "But I can't blame her. She'd written Jim off as a lost cause, but I knew she still loved the guy. If I'd been in her shoes, I probably would have done the same thing."

"Any lost loves in your background?" The question came softly across the shiny tabletop.

"I'm not sure that's any of your business," Stephanie bristled.

"If I'm considering buying a piece of property with you, I think it is," he rejoined calmly. "You just told me you are capable of throwing away everything for love. What if I'm suddenly stuck with two mortgage payments? I warn you, I doubt I'd be as forgiving as you've been with Valerie. I'd have a lawyer filing suit before you took that first step down the aisle."

"I give you my word you don't have to worry about that." She could speak with conviction. Unlike Jim, Gary would never come back and beg her to marry him. Too late she discovered his philosophy about marriage. An "anachronistic custom," he had called it the night she had made such a fool of herself. Never again would she throw herself at a man's feet.

"What about Jeremy?" Lloyd insisted. "The words I believe I heard were 'practically engaged.' Wouldn't you rather get him to buy Valerie's half?"

Stephanie twisted the paper from her straw around one finger. She had to explain this carefully to keep Jeremy as a buffer between her and this charming stranger. Thank heaven Jeremy was so manageable!

"Jeremy and I have a very open relationship," she began.

"Oh?" One dark eyebrow curved upward.

Damn! That wasn't how she meant it! "I mean, we don't force our ideas on each other." That was better. "He doesn't believe in getting his money tied up in property. He owns some bonds, and someday, when we open a clinic together, I'll use the equity from the mingle and he'll cash in his bonds."

"So he's part of this clinic plan, too?"

"Oh yes, definitely." Why did the prospect of Jeremy as a partner seem suddenly distasteful?

"And in the meantime, he won't mind if you live with another man in this mingle?" Lloyd's continued skepticism was wearing a raw place on her already frayed nerves.

"My goodness, you make it sound as if we're doing something illicit!" She forced a tiny laugh. "Each of us would have our own bedroom and bath, and we can lead totally separate lives." She wondered if she was trying to convince him or herself? "I don't know about you, but I'm very busy. We'll probably never see each other."

"Unless we choose to." Lloyd's tawny eyes seemed to evaluate what her bulky sweat shirt concealed.

A male chauvinist after all, she thought, trying to summon her usual righteous indignation as he calmly appraised her. Instead she found herself warming, responding to the suggestion in his eyes. She gulped and dropped her eyes. "Yes, unless we choose to," she mumbled.

"What's the next step, Stephanie?"

"What?" She raised her head in surprise. The amusement twitching the corners of his mouth told her he *meant* to surprise her.

"I think we have a decision to make," he said gently. "What do you think we should do?"

She struggled against her vulnerability. "I'll be honest with you, Lloyd. If you don't buy Valerie's half of the mingle, I'll probably have to give the place up. Marge informed me buyers don't grow on trees in these economic times. However, having you as co-owner is not the solution I would have chosen."

He laughed shortly. "You are a blunt little thing, aren't you? I guess we're even, though, because the last thing in the world I want is a woman as a living partner. I had enough of that when I was married."

"Then perhaps we should forget it." She sighed, remembering the sparkle of the sun on the water, the smell of the salt air filtering through her bedroom door. She always wondered, even when she and Valerie closed the deal, if it was a dream that would never come true. Apparently it was.

"Not necessarily." His words brought up her head with a jerk. "If I had never stood on that balcony, I could kiss this idea goodbye without a single regret." His eyes lingered on her face for a moment. "Well, perhaps with one regret."

Stephanie watched him silently, afraid his thoughts had taken the same direction as hers. She must not let this attraction she felt sabotage all her careful plans. But without Lloyd, those plans were doomed, anyway!

"That view is something I've wanted all my life," he continued. "Even my office at Scripps doesn't have one like it. It's fantastic."

"Yes, it is."

"I'm probably a damn fool for even considering this." He raked his fingers through his dark hair. "What do you think, Stephanie?"

What did she think? She thought it was the riskiest, most foolhardy thing she'd ever done, but what choice did she have? The alternative was ten years of scrimping and living in a dingy apartment.

"I think we should give it a try," she said firmly.

"Me, too." His eyes held hers and she felt suddenly short of breath. What was she doing? What would she tell her parents, whose middle-class attitude surely would not accept their daughter living in a mingle with a man? And there was Sigmund. She had forgotten him completely until this moment, but that little revelation could wait.

2

"YOU'RE DISPLACING, STEPH. Displacing." The hoarse voice croaked clinical advice from the corner of the bedroom as Stephanie, clad in wear-softened jeans and bandanna print top, struggled to center an Andrew Wyeth print on the wall.

"Shut up, Sigmund. If he weren't as nervous as I am, he'd be here by now. But I'm glad he's not. God, if only I could have afforded to buy this all by myself!"

Just a week before she and Lloyd had shared cheeseburgers and decided to live together, but Stephanie had packed a lifetime of worry into those seven days. Live together! She must be out of her mind. Convinced she would wake up from this crazy dream, she had watched Marge orchestrate the necessary paperwork in record time. Valerie stayed in town long enough to sign everything, then left for Illinois with Jim. Their wedding would be at Christmas time, but Stephanie knew she could not afford to fly back for it, and Valerie was forced to choose one of Jim's sisters as her maid of honor. *Life is full of compromises these days*, Stephanie reflected, returning her attention to her picture-hanging chore.

A glancing blow off her thumbnail made her drop the rock she was using for a hammer. She sucked her bruised thumb, wanting to cry or swear and not sure if either offered much consolation. Her clock radio registered noon, and still no sign of Lloyd. If he did not show up soon, she planned to rearrange her meager living-room furniture without him, and he would just have to accept her decisions! Viciously she pounded at the nail again, and in a whoosh of sound it broke through the wallboard and flattened against the plaster. "Damn, no stud," she swore softly.

"Damn stud, damn stud," echoed Sigmund cheerfully.

"Sigmund, I may wring your neck before this is all over, no matter how much you're supposed to be worth. After all, you're still only a—"

A key turning in the back-door lock arrested her in midsentence. "Oh, Sigmund, he's here." Dropping the rock to the floor once more, she wiped her suddenly moist palms against her jeans.

"Anybody home?" His warm voice coursed through her, filling the secret dark places of her soul. It was going to be worse than she imagined. Too late.

Before she could answer, an ear-splitting shriek shattered the silence.

"Stephanie? My God, are you all right? What—" He burst into the bedroom holding a large cardboard carton, alarm widening his eyes. The screech came again, and he spun in the direction of the awful noise.

"A parrot?" It was more accusation than question. "You definitely did not say you had a parrot." His tawny eyes blazed with anger as he faced her, still holding the box.

"It's a scarlet macaw," she said wearily, wondering why she had ever imagined this arrangement would work.

"Whatever. It doesn't matter. What does matter is the terrible sound it makes. You'll have to get rid of it."

"Are you serious? You seem to forget Sigmund and I were here first!" Unconsciously she moved between Lloyd and the bird in a protective gesture. "Besides, that macaw is worth three thousand dollars!"

"Not to me, it's not. It goes." His eyes narrowed with suspicion. "If you're so broke, what are you doing with such a valuable bird?"

Defiantly she returned his angry glare, considering whether to give him any explanation at all. Upset as she was, a part of her brain recognized the blatant sexuality of the man as he stood before her, his legs braced wide apart in a belligerent stance, his dark hair tousled by the ocean breeze. The box he held must be heavy, she thought, because his well-developed biceps strained against the sleeves of his fawn-colored sweat shirt.

"Would you like to put the box down while we talk?" she suggested, and was rewarded with a slight red flush creeping up his neck.

"I guess so," he mumbled, depositing his burden

on the floor. "Now where did you get this obnoxious bird?"

Sigmund tilted his crimson head, regarding them with yellow eyes. "Study the ego; study the id. One is clear; one is hid," he croaked happily, then turned his attention to preening his brilliant red, yellow and blue feathers with a powerful hooked beak.

"Oh, no," Lloyd groaned. "He talks, too."

"Of course," Stephanie snapped. "He's very intelligent, and quite tame. Until he gets used to his new surroundings, I'll keep him penned up—" she waved at the five-foot-high, square stainless-steel cage "—but he's accustomed to roaming free."

"Great." Lloyd seemed thoroughly disgusted, then brightened slightly. "Doesn't he try to fly out the door when you open it?" he asked hopefully, and Stephanie sensed a plot hatching.

"Don't try it, Lloyd," she warned. "Besides, Sigmund's too attached to me. I doubt if he'd leave unless he got very upset about something." A dangerous light glowed in her blue eyes. "And he'd better not get upset."

"What did you call him? Sigmund?"

"Sigmund Freud. I presume you've heard of him?"

"Uh, huh. Cute." He stared balefully at the crimson-headed bird. "I still don't understand why you have a three-thousand-dollar pet. Are you bird-sitting for your friend Jeremy?"

"No." She laid a hand on top of the silver cage.

"Sigmund is all mine. But I didn't buy him. He was given to me."

"By a man," Lloyd guessed correctly.

"Yes." Stephanie smiled, remembering old Mr. Staten, owner of the fast-food chain where she earned money for graduate school. No one warned her that he made incognito visits to the restaurants, or that he rewarded helpful employees in strange ways. Later she heard the stories: the bus boy who cheerfully cleaned up Staten's spilled coke got maid service for five years; the cashier who politely refused his huge tip received a trip around the world. Unaware of his identity, Stephanie listened patiently to Staten's long-winded conversation the day he appeared at her restaurant, and the following week Sigmund arrived in a crate on her doorstep.

"This is just wonderful." Lloyd stomped over to the cage and peered into Sigmund's bright yellow eyes. "Now I'm supposed to put up with noise, and feathers, and Lord knows what else; all because some misguided lover wanted you to remember him forever. Does Sigmund whisper sweet nothings in your ear?"

"Hardly," Stephanie chuckled.

"And what happened to this former boyfriend? Or did Jeremy dream up this charming token of esteem?"

"It wasn't really a boyfriend, Lloyd," Stephanie said, laughing now. "It was an old man who—"

Lloyd held up his hand. "I don't think I even want to know. It sounds too complicated for my present state of befuddlement. But Stephanie—" he faced her squarely "—you should have told me about this bird last week."

"I thought of him after we agreed to buy the mingle together," she admitted. "Frankly, I was afraid if I tried to explain a forty-inch talking macaw, you'd back out." She dropped her eyes, noticing in the process that his fingers rested only inches from hers on the top of the cage. His fingernails were clean and squared off neatly. She liked that.

"After that motorcycle ride, even a forty-inch talking macaw wouldn't have driven me away, Stephanie."

"What?" Startled, she glanced up and met his gaze. What she saw there sent a paralyzing numbness through her system.

"I think you've got the wrong idea, Lloyd," she forced through frozen lips. "This mingle is an investment for me which you are helping make possible. That's all. I do not intend to let our relationship become something else!"

"Stephanie, don't jump to—"

"I will not be your live-in bed partner," she bit out, "and we'd better get that straight right now!"

"Oh, Stephanie." His words came out as a sigh, caressing her although his hands remained at his sides. "Don't you know I'm as afraid of this attraction between us as you are? I've told myself a million times that I'm doing this so I can live by the ocean. But each time I've known it's not just the ocean pulling me here."

"You're making a mistake, Lloyd. It won't work this way. We've got to keep—"

"I've told myself that, too."

She felt the stir of air as his hand moved upward and smoothed the slight crease in her forehead. His touch. She had been waiting for it all week without realizing it. She squeezed her eyes shut, trying to block out the pleasure.

"Don't frown, Stephanie. Don't fight it. You feel it too, don't you? I didn't think I misread the messages of your body against mine last week. If we'd gone to lunch in a car, I might not have known so soon."

"You're wrong," she whispered.

"I'm not wrong." His finger moved down the bridge of her upturned nose to trace the outline of her parted lips. "You want me, too. But you don't know what to do about it, because Jeremy's supposed to be the one for you, isn't he? Not some divorced marine biologist with alimony payments hanging like an albatross around his neck." He shook his head in a rueful gesture. "I know this feeling developed quickly, but sometimes it happens that way. You can try to live your life inside the lines if you want to, but I think you should consider this."

In one swift motion his hand dropped and encircled her waist, pulling her across the short space between them.

"No! You've got no right! I—"

Her protests fluttered ineffectively against the pressure of his mouth. Engulfed in the smothering softness of his sweatshirt-covered arms, she squirmed to free herself, but he held her firmly, his tongue parting her lips and teeth to demand the response she could already feel welling up inside her.

With an anguished groan, she wrenched free, desperately fighting the emotions he loosed in her. "Lloyd! I don't want this," she wailed. "Please leave me alone."

He dropped his arms to his sides, but she saw the clenched fists and recognized the tight control in his voice when he spoke.

"Okay, Stephanie. I've never forced myself on a woman, and I'm not about to start with you. Maybe I was wrong about your reaction to me."

"Wrong!" squawked Sigmund.

"And as for your fine feathered friend," he continued, jabbing a finger in Sigmund's direction, "he'd better keep his comments to himself if he doesn't want to end up simmering in barbecue sauce!" Grabbing his heavy carton as if it was filled with nothing but air, Lloyd stalked from the room, leaving Stephanie a quivering mass of confusion.

She didn't even know Lloyd Barclay! She'd met him for the first time last week! Yet something in her knew him, recognized him with a primitive instinct she could not control. The crush of his lips was familiar; she knew the feel of his skin against hers, how he would love her with gentle urgency, the smell of him, the—no! He was as wrong for her as Jeremy was right. He had the power to destroy her bid for independence. She feared him, feared the ache he inspired. Even Gary, the only man she

had not been able to resist, had not affected her
with this compelling force.

Well, she was older now, stronger. She didn't
have to collapse into a man's arms just because he
raised her pulse a little. She had a plan, and she'd
stick to it. Grimly she returned to the task of
mounting the Wyeth print on the wall, laughing
mirthlessly at the pastoral scene of rusty milk cans
filled with daisies and weathered wagon wheels
leaning against an old barn. Such serenity seemed
ludicrously out of place in this apartment.

The doorbell chimed as she finished adjusting
the picture frame over the brass headboard of her
bed. Good old Jeremy. Valerie had predicted he'd
arrive after the heavy work was done and had gen-
erously loaned Jim's strong back.

Lloyd wasn't responding to the doorbell, she
noted with irritation. The caller might be for
him—although she felt certain it was Jeremy. Impatiently she hurried through the entryway and
yanked open the door.

"You look a little spaced out, Steph," Jeremy
greeted her casually. "Guess I'm just in time with
this." He held up a bottle of wine. "Housewarming
present."

"Your timing is amazing, Jeremy. I've spent the
entire week wrestling stuff from my old apartment
to this place, and you've been mysteriously absent.
How come?" Her anger grew as she remembered
all the packing she'd done, lugging the endless
boxes of books, and wrestling with the impossible
bulk of Sigmund's cage.

"I've been busy with papers to grade. Sorry." A lazy grin lit his soft childlike features. His light hair, curling in wisps around his temples, completed the picture of an overgrown toddler. Stephanie compared the almost pudgy contours of Jeremy's five-foot-ten frame to the muscled hardness she recently experienced in Lloyd's arms. No wonder she'd been able to avoid Jeremy's bed so easily.

"Likely story, Jer," Stephanie snorted.

"You love me for my mind, not my brawn, remember?" He sauntered into the apartment. "Can I make it up to you with some vintage bubbly? It's the best wine $3.98 can buy." He waggled the green bottle in front of her face.

"Jeremy, you're impossible," she said, chuckling, unable to hold her anger long around him. "I still have some unpacking to do, and a couple of glasses of that might make me decide to give up for the day."

"So? It's a gorgeous afternoon. Why not come down to the beach with me? I sense some compulsion in your behavior, Dr. Collier. Relax! What're you trying to do, impress your new roommate?"

Stephanie colored. "Not on your life! I'm just too busy to play, Jer."

"Hmm." Jeremy rubbed his rounded chin. "Had an altercation with the marine biologist already?" His pale blue eyes regarded her curiously.

"You might say that." She rubbed the back of her neck, trying to ease the tightening muscles.

"What about?"

Stephanie hesitated, unwilling to tell the whole

story. "Sigmund," she said at last. "He gave a couple of his famous screeches, and Lloyd came unglued."

"Good old Sigmund." Jeremy grinned appreciatively. "I knew I could count on him in a pinch. Hey, Sigmund, want to go to the beach?"

Sigmund's response was another eardrum-piercing cry, and Stephanie cringed.

"Is there some way we can keep that bird quiet?" Lloyd tore out of his bedroom, then stopped when he saw Jeremy. "Oh. I forgot about the doorbell. Sorry if I sounded rude, but that Sigmund's going to take some getting used to." He looked anything but apologetic.

"He'll grow on you," remarked Jeremy, his pale eyes evaluating Lloyd, then shifting with a worried expression to Stephanie.

He knows, thought Stephanie frantically. *He can tell something's gone on between Lloyd and me.* "Lloyd, this is Jeremy Hammond," she said a little breathlessly. "Jeremy, Lloyd Barclay."

"Glad to meet you," said Jeremy, shaking hands unenthusiastically. "Stephanie tells me you're a marine biologist. Ever gone scuba diving in the cove?"

"Often, as a matter of fact. That was one of the attractions of buying this place." He shifted uncomfortably, as if wanting to ease out of the conversation, but Jeremy held him with another question.

"Is there really lots to see down there? Seems like a lot of trouble and expense, when you could watch

Jacques Cousteau on television and have a cold beer at the same time."

"There's no comparison between pictures and the real thing," Lloyd answered, barely disguising his impatience.

"If that's true, and with Steph living so close to the cove, maybe I'll try a little scuba diving myself."

"Better take some lessons and get certified first," Lloyd warned. "It can be dangerous down there."

"Surely you're not trotting out the old *Jaws* syndrome?" Jeremy scoffed.

"No, not really. The most dangerous creature to man is himself, or *herself*." He glanced pointedly at Stephanie. "Keep forgetting our feminist friend, here."

Stephanie compressed her lips into a stiff line, refusing to voice the retort he expected.

"Anyway," Lloyd continued, "divers often take needless chances by not checking equipment, diving too deep, diving alone, things like that."

"I see. You're one of those thorough and conscientious types, then?"

Stephanie knew from the mocking tone of the questions that Jeremy was spoiling for a chance to upset Lloyd's composure.

"I guess I am," responded Lloyd cheerfully, refusing to rise to the bait.

"Then you should get along just fine with Steph, who is about as compulsive as they come. She won't even share a loaf of bread and a jug of wine with me on the beach."

"I'm sorry, Jeremy, but I really have to get this done." From the corner of her eye she glimpsed Lloyd's surprised expression. "Maybe next weekend?" she found herself saying.

"Sure, why not?" Jeremy's anger pinched his round face, but he managed a smile. "I'll just leave the wine here for another time, and the two of you can work yourselves to death." He plopped the bottle on the counter and left, closing the door with a loud thud behind him.

"I don't think your boyfriend cares for me," Lloyd offered.

"Why should he, after your attitude? You were barely polite," she shot back.

"I guess I didn't take an instant liking to him, either."

"Well, the least you could do is try to be civil." She felt angrier than the episode justified. Was it because the contrast between Lloyd and Jeremy pointed up all of Jeremy's inadequacies?

Suddenly Lloyd grinned. "Hey, let's not fight again. Although I must admit you're cute all riled up like that. You remind me of a kitten I had once who faced down a Saint Bernard. That little ball of fluff was fearless, arching her back and spitting at the huge monster in front of her." His eyes softened to the color of caramel candy. "She was also the most loving pet I've ever owned."

"Is that how you think of women, too? As pets?" she accused.

"No, of course not, my feminist fireball. I'm only trying to say I admire your spirit, Stephanie." His golden eyes penetrated the depths of her blue ones for a moment longer before he turned and walked into his bedroom.

Stephanie stood stock still for several seconds, then shook her head as if to clear it. "Damn," she said softly, then wandered back to her room to tackle the rest of the unpacking.

Maybe she shouldn't have given up the chance to drink wine on the beach. The idea sounded pretty good. Still, the week of piecemeal moving was nearly over, and this evening she could finally sleep in the bedroom she had worked so hard to get. She plunged into the last few tasks.

An hour of solid effort produced a semblance of order to the room. After smoothing her grandmother's quilt over the freshly made bed and adjusting the shade on the white hobnail lamp on her bedside table, she decided to drive to the grocery store. The living-room arrangement would have to wait. She had seen no evidence of Lloyd's furniture, so they would have to figure out the common areas later.

A rented moving truck sat in the parking lot next to her Chevette, and she eyed it with envy, remembering all the trips it had taken to transfer her belongings from her old apartment. Careful of every penny, she had decided against renting a truck, but her aching muscles from the past week had told her she might have made an error in judgment. Anyway, it was done. With a tiny sigh, she slipped behind the steering wheel of her small car.

When she returned some time later with a bulging shopping bag in each arm, neither the moving truck nor the black motorcycle were in Lloyd's assigned parking space. Struggling with a mixture of regret and relief, she pushed the button on the elevator outside the building with her elbow. She had vowed not to make a habit of riding the elevator the four floors to the apartment, but today she needed a touch of luxury.

Back in the kitchen, she put away her small stockpile of groceries, carefully labeling each item with an *S.C.* Then she decided on a long hot shower before dinner. As the warm water worked the kinks of tension from her neck and shoulders, she thought again of Lloyd. Would he eat his supper at home? Realizing he might, she took the precaution of dressing in fresh jeans and a warm sweat shirt instead of throwing on a robe, as she would have done if she were living with Valerie. Damn the inconvenience! Fluffing her damp curls with her fingers, she started toward the kitchen to prepare a light supper.

"Suppertime," sounded a forlorn voice behind her.

"I'm sorry, Sigmund. It's time for you to eat, too, isn't it? One ration of sunflower seeds, coming right up. And I bought some fresh fruit at the store." As she walked toward the cage to retrieve his food cup, a white piece of paper tied to the handle at the top of the cage caught her attention. Unfastening the twist tie, she opened the folded paper and read in astonishment.

Dear Stephanie,
After what's happened, you probably think of
me as some sort of uncontrolled animal. Believe me when I tell you that nothing will happen between us unless we both want it. You
are perfectly safe with me.
Lloyd

Stephanie held the note, rereading it several
times. The words brought back the touch of Lloyd's
hand, the pressure of his lips on hers. Safe? She
hardly thought so, although it wasn't Lloyd she
feared, but herself.

"I don't know about all this, Sigmund," she said
softly.

"Pretty Stephanie, pretty Stephanie," chortled the
rainbow-colored bird, fluffing his brilliant feathers.

"Where did you pick that up, you crazy fellow?"
The thought occurred to her that Lloyd might have
taught him to say it, but it seemed too unlikely. He
didn't even like the bird.

The unexpected note succeeded in focusing her
thoughts on Lloyd for the rest of the evening, and
each sound of footsteps outside the door acceler-
ated her heartbeat. By ten o'clock, as she lay
propped in bed studying lecture notes for the next
day's classes, she decided he was staying away on
purpose.

"And I certainly am not going to wait up for him
like some dorm mother," she told Sigmund with a
wry grin, reaching to switch off her bedside lamp.
"Good night, Sigmund."

"Good night, Stephanie," croaked the scarlet-plumed bird.

Although physically exhausted from an unsettling week, Stephanie found sleep an elusive commodity. She tried all the relaxation routines she knew, but still she lay wide awake, listening for a key in the lock.

"Damn it, Sigmund. I wouldn't be doing this if Valerie were out late," she said into the darkness. Her only answer was a drowsy croak. "I'm glad you can sleep," she muttered. "I'm going to have to lick this or be a walking zombie tomorrow." She forced herself to concentrate on the muffled surge of the waves. During the week she had bought a dowel cut the right size to fit in the track of her balcony door. It allowed an inch of sea air and ocean sounds to penetrate her bedroom solitude, yet discouraged intruders. Intruders, hah! The intruder she would like to keep out already had a key to the place. *Enough of that,* she reminded herself sternly. She *had* to get some sleep. Curling into a ball, she focused on the repetitive sound of the waves, like the rustle of taffeta against a polished dance floor...swish...swish....

An intense white light, followed closely by an explosive crash and Sigmund's blood-curdling shriek, jolted Stephanie from her bed. Shaking violently, she stood in the middle of the floor, her sleep-fogged mind trying to assess the danger. A second flash of light, followed by another crash, drew her gaze through the sliding doors to the ocean, where a storm marched on lightning-bolt legs across the horizon, churning the sea into a frenzy, sending white-capped waves fifteen feet into the air before they plummeted against the rocky shore. The tall palms in the grassy park bent before the force of the wind, waving their broad fronds in frantic supplication.

"My God." Stephanie's eyes widened in fright. She never had been so close to an ocean storm, and this one promised to be violent.

"Good morning, Stephanie." Sigmund's cheerful greeting made her giggle nervously.

"It's not morning, you silly old bird. I only hope we're not getting hit by some sort of tropical hurricane." She shivered as the cool air from the crack in the door engulfed her thinly clad body. Her lacy white negligee reached just below her hips, and the chill breeze raised goose bumps on her bare arms and legs. "Come on, Sigmund; let's turn on the radio and see if we've got anything to be worried ab—" A deafening peal of thunder and the glare of lightning drowned out the end of her sentence and sent her bounding under the covers in terror as Sigmund screeched again.

"Stephanie?" Lloyd's voice called through the closed bedroom door, and in her need for reassurance, Stephanie leaped from her bed and flung open the door.

His large frame loomed in the doorway, soothing her jangled nerves. A dark Oriental-style robe was belted loosely at his waist and hung down to bare knees. Apparently, the man didn't wear pajamas.

"I heard the commotion in here, and I thought you might be afraid." His voice contained none of the anger she might have expected, considering Sigmund's raucous reaction to the storm, and she smiled gratefully. Pajamas or no pajamas, she was glad not to be alone at this moment.

"Is it a se-serious storm?" Her teeth chattered slightly as she spoke.

"No. I was at Scripps tonight, and they don't expect anything more than a few fireworks and some high waves. Aren't you cold?" His eyes surveyed her scantily clothed body, and she blessed the darkened room, knowing it hid something of her form and the blush she felt rising in her cheeks.

"Not really. I—" Thunder shook the glass door, and instinctively Stephanie catapulted into Lloyd's arms, burying her head against the reassuring warmth of his chest in an attempt to drown out the receding rumbles from the storm-torn sky. Silk. The robe was silk. And where it gaped open in front, springy hairs tickled her cheek. She felt his arms tighten around her and a sense of safety began to replace her fright.

"This kind of storm is really something for a midwestern girl," she mumbled against his chest. "I guess you must think I'm a first-class scaredy cat, huh?"

"Not at all." The sound of his voice vibrated against her skin, soothing her. "I grew up here, and I still find a heavy storm at sea quite a sight. This one shouldn't be too bad, but once in a while we get one that claims lives. A healthy fear isn't all bad. What always helped me, though, was to understand how the storm works. Do you know anything about meteorology?''

''Not much,'' she whispered against his chest, wondering if she imagined an increased tempo in his heartbeat. Her own heart was thudding rapidly as she felt her body begin to react to his, but she hated to leave the safety of his arms.

''Then let's sit down and I'll tell you a little about the mechanics of this storm.'' He led her to the rumpled bed, where they both sat on the edge facing the glass door and the pyrotechnics beyond it. As he talked of sea and air currents, temperatures and tides, Lloyd kept his arm loosely around her shoulders, his fingers tracing a feathery pattern along her upper arm.

''You have a special affinity for the ocean, don't you?'' Stephanie said, trying to ignore the warm current of feeling his feather touch stirred in her.

''Yes.'' He kept his eyes on the tossing waves. ''It's one of the most majestic natural forces I know. It may sound corny, but I'm inspired by the immensity and the power of that surging water.''

''Does it ever frighten you?''

''Of course.'' He looked at her then, the kindness in his face barely discernible in the darkness. ''Only fools wouldn't have a great respect for that kind of power, Stephanie. Don't be ashamed by your fear.''

''It's pretty dumb, isn't it? I'm a psychologist who helps other people overcome their fears, yet I'm not ready to overcome mine.''

He chuckled, a warm sound in the chill of the

room. "Sort of like the doctors who won't admit to being sick. Happens all the time, I guess."

"Well, I feel much better after your explanation, Lloyd. Thanks." It was a cue, a signal for him to leave her room, and he sensed it. He dropped his arm.

Fighting a feeling of loss, Stephanie stood up. "I guess we'd better get some sleep. It must be late."

"About two o'clock, I think." Lloyd stood up beside her. A sudden flash of lightning bathed them both in white light, revealing to Lloyd everything the dimness of the room had hidden.

"Stephanie." His voice was a dry rasp, and Stephanie's breath caught at the desire she heard in each syllable of her name. "Damn it, woman," he said shakily. "I do wish you had more clothes on."

"You're not so completely covered, yourself," she said lightly, trying to ease the tension.

"That's right." Repressed emotion laced his voice tight. "I sleep in the nude and I didn't take time for the amenities when I heard the noise in here."

Stephanie gasped as images of Lloyd's lithe form bombarded her senses.

"Did I shock you, Stephanie? Better be warned not to come waltzing into my room unannounced. Well, good night and sleep tight." He bent his head and aimed a kiss at her cheek, but an irresistible urge made her turn her head and his lips landed directly on hers.

She felt his sharp intake of breath before he gathered her with a groan into his arms. *Now I've done it,* she thought, as the dizzying force of his kiss drew all resistance from her and she allowed herself to be pulled against him.

The sheer nylon of her gown shielded little of the impact as her breasts flattened against the hard wall of his chest. She felt her nipples pucker under the thin material, knew he could feel it, too.

Already his tongue sought the warm recesses of her mouth and one large hand molded her hips against the soft silk of his robe, where she could easily feel his arousal. Slowly releasing her lips, he nuzzled past the gold hoop of her earring to trail soft, nipping kisses down the slender column of her neck.

"What a surprise, Stephanie," he crooned, his breath hot against her skin. "I planned to leave like a gentleman tonight, but you wouldn't let me do that, would you?" Gently he pushed aside the thin strap of her nightgown as his lips moved along her shoulder.

Stephanie fought the urge to arch against him, to invite the next step in his seduction. She pulled away slightly. "Lloyd, I'm sorry. I don't know what made me do that. I didn't mean—"

"Oh, I think you did, Stephanie." The small distance she placed between them opened new areas of exploration to Lloyd's questing fingers, and he traced the lacy scallop of her neckline to the hollow between her breasts. "Can't you tell how natural this feels, how right?"

It was true, Stephanie realized. When he first

drew her against him, her arms found their way instinctively, and her hands of their own volition kneaded the muscles of his back.

"But I hardly know you!" she protested, acutely aware of his fingers moving under her gown to caress the satiny skin of her breast.

"You know me, Stephanie," he whispered. "You've been waiting for someone like me all your life. Do you imagine you can be happy in bed with a man you can manage like a puppet?"

"Jeremy's not a puppet!"

"No? Then why hasn't he slept with you?"

"Because I—" She stopped, confused. "You don't know that!"

"Yes, I do. A woman has a certain air when she's around a man she's been to bed with. When Jeremy was here this afternoon, you didn't have it."

"Are you such an expert on these things?" She trembled as his hand dropped lower to cup her breast, but she felt helpless to stop him.

"Not an expert. Just aware. Strange that you're 'practically engaged' to someone who has never done this...." His thumb flicked against her nipple. "Or this...." Pushing the material away, he bent his head to take the stiffened tip in his teeth.

Stephanie thought her heart had stopped beating. "Perhaps he's more of a gentleman than you," she gasped. She heard her absent heartbeat. It thundered in her ears as Lloyd's tongue circled and teased, sending tremors through her heated body.

"I hope so," he murmured. "I certainly hope so." He released his firm hold on her hips to push the nightgown top past her waist and over her thighs until the gown drifted silently to the floor. The lightning flashed again and she read the passion in his golden eyes.

"Beautiful." The word fell around her like a cloak as she stood swaying slightly in front of him. "You're beautiful, Stephanie."

He held her only with his eyes. *I'm free to stop him*, she thought wonderingly. Lloyd wanted the final decision to be hers. Her heart clattered in tempo with the thunder outside her door as she wavered. Her body wanted him—the growing ache in her loins told her that—but what of tomorrow? What of next week, next year? Would she be able to sell her half of the mingle and walk away?

"Come to me, Stephanie."

"Lloyd, I think we're making a mistake...."

"Loving is never a mistake, Stephanie. Let me show you. Tomorrow will take care of itself. We need each other tonight." His voice drew her magically closer. "Come." He held out his hand and slowly she placed her own in it. The palm of her hand registered the hardened callouses at the base of his fingers, the strength of his grip as his hand tightened over hers, pulling her down with him onto the rumpled bed.

"Good morning, Stephanie!" The voice sounded clearly in the darkness.

"What the h—" Lloyd jumped from the bed. "Who's there?"

Bolting upright, Stephanie realized in horror what had happened. "That was Sigmund," she choked out, her heart beating like a trip-hammer.

"The bird?" Lloyd's voice registered disbelief. "But it sounded just like a person!"

"He's capable of that sometimes." She gulped for air. Suddenly the room felt cold, and she pulled the sheet tightly around her.

"Sigmund, I'd like to wring your neck," Lloyd muttered, advancing threateningly on the cage.

"Don't you dare touch that bird!"

"Good morning, good morning," croaked Sigmund cheerfully, hopping from perch to perch.

"Maybe it still can be, no thanks to you," Lloyd addressed the bird. "Don't worry, Stephanie." He turned back to her. "I wouldn't really...hey, what are you doing huddled under the covers?"

"Lloyd, I think you'd better go," she answered miserably. The spell was broken.

"On second thought, I just may murder that bird," said Lloyd in amazement. "I think Sigmund just ruined what could have been a beautiful moment in our lives, Stephanie."

"I'm sorry, Lloyd, but I'm not willing to trade my whole future for a single moment, no matter how beautiful."

"Is that right? That's not the impression I got before Big Mouth over here got wound up."

"I forgot myself." Stephanie hugged the sheet around her quaking body, trying to ignore the hurt in his voice.

"And didn't realize what you were doing? Come on, Stephanie! You're a big girl now, and responsible for your actions. But far be it for me to try and

change your mind now. I'm going to bed...alone."
He stalked out of the room.

After she heard his bedroom door slam, she continued to sit up in bed for several minutes, stunned by the sudden turn of events. How had things progressed so far? Why in the world had she kissed him in the first place? And then, just when she was ready to surrender everything, Sigmund....

All at once she pictured the scene as it must have looked, and a tiny crinkle appeared at the corner of her mouth. The crinkle became a broad smile, followed by a chuckle, and finally, whoops of mirth, which she smothered in her pillow. She laughed until the tears came and her sides ached. Slowly the chuckles subsided, and she lay on her back, gasping, listening to the ping of the rain against the wrought-iron balcony railing.

The laughter had erased the tension from her body, but her mind could not ignore the complications this night had created in her life. Neither did she feel like sorting everything out, as the steady drip of the rain lulled her into heavy-lidded drowsiness. Now seemed the time to use the problem-solving technique she taught her students; she would deliver the whole mess to her subconscious to unravel as she slept.

"So go at it in there," she mumbled to her inner self. "I expect an answer in the morning."

"Good night, Stephanie," rasped a familiar voice from the corner of the room.

Stephanie smiled sleepily. "Good night, Sigmund."

3

CAUTIOUSLY STEPHANIE PUSHED HER GROCERY CART down the supermarket aisle, determined to keep her presence a secret from Lloyd, who lurked in the next aisle. But one wheel of her cart squeaked, giving her away. He rounded the frozen food case and spied her. Quickly she spun her cart and dashed down the cake-and-cookie aisle, but the dry wheel signaled her direction. She ran faster as his footsteps chased her toward the cash registers. Should she abandon the cart? No, she needed the jumble of groceries it carried. Squeak, squeak, squeak protested the dry wheel. He closed the distance between them, reaching for her before she could enter the safety of the checkout lane....

Stephanie snapped awake, her heart racing. She could still hear the noise of the cart! A flash of gray and white arced through the blue sky beyond her balcony, and the high-pitched sound came again. A gull.... She collapsed against her pillow, grinning. What an imagination her subconscious had! She had no trouble interpreting the dream, but it didn't seem to contain the answers she had ordered before she went to sleep.

The aroma of freshly perked coffee reminded her

that although her supermarket chase was imaginary, she had her share of real problems with the person brewing that coffee. How could she face him after what happened the night before? What a disastrous beginning! And if Sigmund had not interrupted, she might be waking this morning in Lloyd's arms. No might about it, she admitted honestly, remembering how easy it had been to melt into his embrace. Even now, the memory made her flush hot with embarrassment, but there was another emotion jockeying for position, too. A telltale quiver of desire told her she still wanted him. Oh, Lord, what now? She was falling under his spell just as she had with Gary, and that could only mean heartbreak.

The previous night's storm had ripped away her defenses, but she was determined to rebuild them. Propping herself on one elbow, she stared spellbound at the placid scene that had replaced the ferocity of only a few hours before. The angry waves had vanished, leaving gentle iridescent swells topped here and there with plumes of white foam glistening like stray bits of shaving cream. On the grassy expanse of the adjacent park, a jogger in a cardinal-red sweat suit followed the winding cement path skirting the cove.

"Fantastic," she whispered, swinging bare legs over the edge of the bed and standing to get a better view of the shoreline panorama. "I can't let a screwed-up love affair ruin this for us, Sigmund," she continued with determination. What in the world had come over her the night before? She had to make sure it did not happen again, even if a full-blown hurricane hit La Jolla, she vowed, padding barefoot to the bathroom.

Stephanie did her most creative thinking in the shower—the hot steam loosened both her mental and physical muscles. Scrubbing her skin vigorously with the washcloth, she concentrated on the problem of Lloyd Barclay.

Attractive though he was—and she had to admit the chemistry between them was powerful—he could only mean trouble. She wanted to live in this mingle on her own timetable, selling when the market was right instead of when a love affair soured. She had watched office romances, seen the pain when two people were forced to work side by side after a relationship ended. How much worse to have to live with a former lover!

Somehow she had to convince Lloyd of her indifference to his charms. Considering her unbridled response the previous night, he might try again, once his bruised ego healed.

She had to develop the strength to refuse him! Spending more time with Jeremy would help, and Sigmund could be a continuing barrier, just as he inadvertently had been the night before. Lloyd didn't care for the bird, and by lavishing love and time on Sigmund, she might throw up roadblocks to their sensual attraction, an attraction that threatened all her careful plans.

Toweling off with rapid strokes, Stephanie hummed softly to herself. She was ready; her goals were clear. Lloyd Barclay had better watch his step from now on!

Quickly she buttoned on a green silk shirt—a gift from her mother—and paired it with green-and-brown plaid slacks. Slipping into brown wedge heels, she decided to leave her makeup off until after breakfast. No point in putting on an alluring face for Lloyd. Smoothing the antique quilt over her bed and promising Sigmund some fresh fruit within the next few minutes, she strode purposefully out of the bedroom, feeling brave and confident.

"You finally decided to get up." He lounged casually on one of a pair of bar stools, the first evidence of his furniture she had seen. She scanned the living room, but saw only her rocker, her cobbler's bench end table and her assortment of throw pillows. The only other objects in the room were her books, lined carefully on pine-board and cinder-block bookshelves.

"My first class isn't until ten," she tossed back defensively, then wished she'd used a lighter tone. "Don't you have any living room furniture?"

"Not yet. My other apartment was furnished. I'm going out this morning to shop."

"But I saw a rented moving truck."

"What I did have didn't fit too well on my motorcycle," he reminded her dryly, then raised his cup. "Want some coffee?"

"Are you offering because it's my coffee you're drinking?" Instantly she regretted the remark. One lousy scoop of coffee hardly made a difference. "I'm sorry. That sounded pretty stingy."

"Sure did, but I understand why you'd be edgy. Picking fights is not going to solve our problem, Stephanie, so let's try to be civil, as you might say."

She registered the weariness in his voice and felt remorse for her sharp tongue. He looked as if he hadn't slept the night before, and she longed to smooth the lines of fatigue around his eyes, to caress the soft knit of the chocolate-brown shirt molded against his powerful chest, to... what was she thinking?

"If we just keep out of each other's way, we won't have a problem," she said stiffly. "At least I won't."

"Won't you? You must realize that all your thoughts show on your cherubic face, so you might as well make up your mind right now never to lie to me, Stephanie." He folded his arms across his chest and regarded her calmly, so sure of himself that she felt like screaming.

She took a deep breath. "Excuse me, but I have to get some fruit for Sigmund," she said carefully, attempting to erase all emotion from her voice as she moved past him toward the refrigerator.

"Just a minute." His fingers closed on the soft silk of her sleeve, and her heart tripped into high gear. She swallowed convulsively, hating the wild reaction of her senses to his touch, and refused to meet his eyes. If he could read her face, she did not want him knowing what she was thinking at the moment!

"All right, I'm standing here." She shook her arm away impatiently. "You don't have to man-handle me to get my attention. What is it?" His nearness still disturbed her, but at least she was free of that electrifying touch.

"I checked your schedule." He jerked his head toward the wall calendar she had tacked up the previous day. "You don't have classes this after-noon, do you?" The motion of his head caused a lock of jet-black hair to fall over his forehead, and she clenched her hands into fists, fighting the im-pulse to smooth the lock of hair back into place.

"That's right. So what?" She sounded belligerent, but she couldn't help it. If she had a choice between that or quivering vulnerability, she'd choose bellig-erence.

"So you're the logical one to stay here and wait for the telephone installer."

"The telephone installer?" She looked at him blankly. "Who arranged for the telephone to be in-stalled?"

"I did." His tone was efficient, businesslike. "I told them we'd need an extension in each bedroom and a double listing in the book, but it's quite a bit cheaper if we both use the same number." He paused, eyeing her speculatively. "Of course, if you'd rather not . . . ."

"It makes sense, of course," she replied stiffly. "That's what this is all about, isn't it? Saving money?" She noticed the sudden gleam in his golden eyes, but he answered in a neutral voice.

"Oh, yes, we want to save money. Which brings

up another subject. You were in that shower more than ten minutes. Twelve, to be exact. We only have one meter, and I plan to take my showers in less than five. Are you prepared to pay a greater share of the electric bill, or will you curtail your long showers?''

Stephanie flushed crimson with anger and embarrassment. How dare he regulate the length of her showers! While she had been in there planning how they might work out this crazy living arrangement, he sat out here sipping her coffee and timing how much hot water she was using!

"Well, which will it be?" He stared at her, his face revealing no emotion.

"Henceforth I will take my alarm clock into the bathroom with me," she flung at him, "unless of course you want to sound a gong outside my door when you think I've used up my quota of hot water." Her blue eyes blazed with fury. Tomorrow, when she had a phone, she would start calling electricians until she came up with one who could install a separate meter. The cost paled in comparison to the alternative—tolerating this infuriating man's interference with one of her most personal pleasures.

"We could save even more money if we showered together," he offered. She gaped, her eyes wide, as he struggled to suppress a smile.

"Not on your life!" she gasped, and watched helplessly as he broke into laughter, the rich sound filling the apartment.

"If you don't mind, I'll get some fruit for Sigmund's breakfast and be on my way." She lifted her chin, determined to salvage a shred of pride.

"What about the telephone installer?" he asked, his laughter subsiding.

"You arranged it. Why can't you be here?" Apparently he felt he could order her around as well!

"I set up the appointment before I knew I had to work in the lab this afternoon. If you can't do it, I'll try to rearrange my schedule. It's important to my work that Scripps be able to call me whenever necessary. I need to get this telephone installed."

"It's important for me, too," Stephanie admitted reluctantly, hating the implication that he had done her a favor by taking the time to make the appointment. "I do a little counseling on the side, and right now no one can get in touch with me. I just hadn't gotten around to contacting the telephone company." She paused, then added honestly, "I guess I should be grateful that you took care of it."

"Don't mention it. Can you be here, then?"

"Yes, I'll do it." She took two firm red apples from the refrigerator and snapped a fragrant banana from the bunch sitting on the counter. "Now, if you'll excuse me, I'll feed Sigmund his breakfast." She did not mention the fruit would provide her meal, as well. In her present mood, she'd probably make a mess of anything she tried to cook. The aroma of the coffee in the still-warm pot beckoned her, but she did not want to remain in the kitchen long enough to pour it.

"Stephanie." His tone softened. "About last night—"

"Let's just forget it, shall we?" She wanted to put the previous night as far behind her as possible, not spend time rehashing the mistake they had almost made.

"I can guarantee that you won't forget it, and neither will I. And just for the record, that was my coffee I offered you. I only take what I believe to be mine. You can count on that."

She glared up at him defiantly, meeting the challenge in his eyes with all the strength she could muster, but the longer she tried, the more she seemed to drown in the topaz depths.

"I have to get going or I'll be late for class," she said at last. She turned and walked from the room, certain that his eyes followed her until she disappeared from his sight.

STEPHANIE'S STOMACH GROWLED UNMERCIFULLY as she fumbled with the door key. She needed some lunch and a few hours of quiet after the strain of shepherding a large beginning psychology class through a maze of conflicting behavior theories. The class contained a handful of promising students, but too many of the group expected an easy three hours' work, a gift Stephanie felt unwilling to give.

Tossing her notebook and purse on the kitchen counter, she rinsed her hands at the kitchen sink, making a mental note to place a bar of soap there. Glancing around she realized she had forgotten to buy paper towels, and her dish towels were still packed. Hands dripping, she ran to her bathroom and grabbed her bath towel, catching a glimpse of herself in the medicine-cabinet mirror as she dried her hands. With a shock she noticed her face was bare of makeup. The confrontation with Lloyd had made her forget to put any on!

"Oh, well, Sigmund," she addressed the colorful bird, who fluttered out of a lazy snooze and regarded her with bright yellow eyes. "I seem to be turning into an absentminded professor, after all, thanks to a certain marine biologist of our acquaintance."

She stuck her tongue out at the face in the mirror, looking more like twelve than twenty-six. Without makeup to mute the splash of freckles across her nose, and with her mop of yellow curls, she looked like a blond Little Orphan Annie, she thought ruefully. Definitely not Lloyd Barclay's type.

Another rumble from her stomach reminded her that her food consumption for the day had consisted of one apple and the portion of a banana she had coaxed from Sigmund. Replacing the fluffy towel on its rack, she walked through her bedroom door toward the kitchen, only then noticing something different about the apartment.

Sitting in the middle of the living room were two of the ugliest pieces of furniture she had ever seen. Tubes of shiny chrome dominated both pieces, some supporting the glass of a coffee table and others forming the base for fat black patent leather cushions, loosely arranged to resemble a chair. Did Lloyd expect to have these stark objects in the same room with her Boston rocker and calico pillows?

She groaned aloud, picturing in advance the wrangling that would assuredly take place as they tried to create some sort of harmony in the room. Eclectic was one thing, but this was too much. Never in her wildest dreams had she imagined he would buy furniture like this, but then, what did she really know about him, other than his job title and the strong evidence that he understood a great deal about how to please a woman in bed?

"And he loves the ocean," she added out loud, aware in a flash of insight that she had based her decision to live with this man on that single fact about him. Hardly enough of an indication of someone's character. And she called herself a psychologist!

Mechanically she fixed an economical lunch, draining the oil from a can of tuna, adding into a bowl a spoonful of mayonnaise and another of tangy pickle relish before spreading part of the concoction on a slice of whole-wheat toast. Hard-boiled eggs would be nice, too, she thought, positioning another slice of toast to complete the sandwich. That was another item to add to her growing list of things to get. How long would it be before she felt settled and at home here? Perhaps never, she admitted, biting into the succulent tuna and taking a sip from a tall glass of cold milk.

Standing at the counter, she watched an oil tanker inch along the line of ocean at the horizon.

Impulsively scooping up her lunch in one hand and dragging her rocker with the other, she moved out to the balcony to eat. When she could afford it, she'd buy a wrought-iron lawn chair, but the rocker had to do for now.

Breathing deeply of the cool salt-laden air, she felt better. This was one of the main reasons she was there, she reminded herself as she enjoyed the play of seawater against the crescent of sand in the cove. Her eyes swept the shoreline, coming to rest unbidden on the Scripps Institute buildings about two miles away, clinging like large barnacles to the beach. Somewhere in one of those buildings Lloyd stood in a white lab coat, his dark head bent over a microscope.

Her stomach churned as she remembered the previous night, and she wondered if Lloyd had thought of it, too. Would they be able to share this mingle, or would the tension between them destroy all her careful plans? She had no idea what the answer would be.

The telephone installer arrived late in the afternoon, but Stephanie found plenty to do, completing the unpacking in the kitchen and putting the finishing touches on her bedroom. She left the living room strictly alone, dreading the confrontation she knew would come. She carefully allotted half of the kitchen cupboard space for Lloyd, although the coffeepot, a can of coffee and one mug were all the supplies he seemed to have. Perhaps he ate out all the time, she reasoned, and experienced a disturbing pang of disappointment.

"Say, lady, what color telephones you want?" The man's voice floated out of Lloyd's bedroom, where he was testing the jack to make sure it worked correctly. "This order here doesn't say color."

"Um, just a minute," Stephanie hedged, unsure whether she dare make such a mundane decision for Lloyd. Why not? He could always change it later. She strolled into his room to assess his color scheme, trying to appear nonchalant yet feeling like the most flagrant trespasser. When she was inside the door, her mouth sagged open.

She should not have been surprised, she told herself. After the chrome-and-black monsters in the living room, what did she expect?

A huge water bed dominated the room. And he had challenged her about hot water? She knew enough about these beds to understand they must be filled with warm water to begin with if the user hopes to sleep there the same night. Seething, she ran her hand over the black leather bolsters of the massive bed and stooped to finger the velvety black spread that resembled a panther's pelt. In addition to the bed, the room contained a black-lacquered chest and nightstand, which stood in bold relief against the room's white plaster. The only spark of color in the room came from a Picasso print on the wall.

"Ugh." The exclamation slipped from Stephanie's lips before she could halt it.

"What was that, ma'am?" The bearded installer glanced up from the jack after tightening the screw on the plastic plate. "What color do you want in here?"

"Black," she replied, maintaining a deadpan expression.

"Okay." The installer made a note on his clipboard, his own face a mask of impersonality. "Don't get many requests for that anymore."

"I'll bet."

"And the other bedroom?" If he wondered at all about the living arrangement—the obviously masculine bedroom and the clearly feminine one linked by a common living area and occupied by two people with different last names—he gave no indication of his curiosity.

"I'll take white," Stephanie said, wishing she could afford a period decorator phone to match her Early American bedroom. But that was out of the question, so white would be the least conspicuous.

After the installer left, Stephanie stood for a moment pondering the advisability of calling her parents. When she had announced her plans to live with a male roommate, her parents' response had been cool. Now, although she knew she needed to tell them her new number, she dreaded the call. The sound of a hand on the doorknob made the choice for her. One battle per night was enough. She would call her parents tomorrow.

"Did the telephone man arrive?" Lloyd edged the door closed with one foot, balancing a brown grocery bag against each lean hip.

"What makes you so sure it was a man?" she bristled.

"Oh. Sorry, *Ms* Collier." He deposited the bags on the counter, the errant lock of hair falling over his forehead again as he bent to remove the contents of the first sack. "Did the telephone *person* arrive?"

"Yes." She ignored the sarcasm in his voice, saving her combative energies for more immediate concerns. "I chose the color of your phone for you."

"Oh? What did you get?" He asked the question absently, his attention on the contents of the bags.

"Black." She could not repress a smile.

His head came up. "I take it you've been in my room, then."

"Yes, I have. Who's your decorator, Darth Vader?"

"Very funny. I happen to like the clean, crisp look of black and white. Any objections?" His tawny eyes held hers captive, and her heart leaped wildly in her chest. She forced herself to focus on the chrome-and-black chair behind him in the living room.

"I may have some objections, but we'll discuss that in a moment. I have another question, a mathematical problem. How many twelve-minute showers does it take to fill a giant water bed?"

He had the decency to redden, but he gave no ground. "That's a one-time expense, and I planned to put in an extra share toward this month's bill. I was talking about what probably is a constant habit on your part."

"And I suppose you don't have any expensive

habits? How about a television? Do you sit in front of the tube watching all that sports stuff on TV? Do you even realize how much electricity that uses?" Her eyes bit into him like steel-blue augers.

"I don't own a television."

"Oh." She digested this amazing piece of information. Besides herself, she did not know anyone who did not have at least a portable black-and-white set. Occasionally, when a special series or movie came on, she regretted not buying one, but ordinarily she filled her leisure time with books and music. Since moving to California, she had added one more activity—long walks by the ocean. "Well, I hope you weren't counting on watching mine," she said suspiciously. "I don't have one either."

"Now I have at least one reason to be glad you're co-owner of this mingle."

Stephanie winced inwardly at his deliberate gibe.

"I was prepared to put up with a TV blaring every evening," he added, returning to the task of unpacking his groceries.

"I guess you're in luck, because the only thing I might have blaring would be a Tchaikovsky symphony or some down-home country music."

He quirked one eyebrow in her direction. "Kind of a strange combination, isn't it?"

"Not any stranger than a decorating scheme in basic black," she shot back, determined not to be intimidated.

"You don't like black." He affected a hurt tone.

"Sure I do—on horses, and limousines, and

draped around funeral caskets. But as a dominant color in a room, I find it very depressing." She glanced pointedly at the patent leather chair.

"You don't like my chair, either, do you?"

"To tell the truth, Lloyd, I don't care for a single piece of furniture you own, but it wouldn't matter about the bedroom. That's up to you." He raised both eyebrows this time and opened his mouth to interrupt, but she rushed on. "The thing is, we have to bring some sort of order to the living room, and I don't see how that's possible with that... that...." She waved expressively at the chair and glass end table, unable to find an appropriate description for the shiny objects.

"Did it ever occur to you," he began, taking a step toward her, "that I might object to your cozy little rocker and cute pillows? Perhaps I'm interested in creating an air of sophistication in this room, and rocking chairs remind me of one thing: grandmothers bent over their knitting!"

"And what's wrong with that?" Her voice reached stridently across the space between them. "I happen to like that image of warmth and caring, two things you obviously know nothing about." Her eyes glittered dangerously.

"You think you have me all figured out, don't you?" He closed the space between them in a single motion, grabbing her by the shoulders. "You may be a psychologist, and you may pride yourself on being able to poke and probe into the innermost feelings of everyone you meet, but watch out when you begin to psychoanalyze me, Stephanie Collier!" His fingers pressed ridges in her shoulders as his eyes burned deeply into her own. The tension between them grew as she met his anger head on, refusing to drop her own fierce gaze. Gradually, the fury in his topaz eyes changed subtly to something else, something that turned the stiff resistance in Stephanie's knees to wobbly indecision.

Lloyd wanted her. Even more frightening to her was the realization that her anger was subsiding as well, to be replaced with a fiery need she remembered only too well. This had to stop! Summoning all her willpower, she wrenched free of his grasp.

"Do whatever you want with the living room," she flung at him. "I'm going out to eat." She grabbed her purse from the kitchen counter and fled the apartment, knowing the night chill would slice through the thin covering of her silk blouse, but also knowing that if she stayed a moment longer, even to get a coat, she would be in Lloyd's embrace.

THE STEEP CLIMB to the commercial area above Coast Boulevard provided a welcome challenge to Stephanie as she trudged doggedly toward the bustle of shops and restaurants. Still flushed from her encounter with Lloyd, she was barely aware of the cool currents of air swirling through the half light of evening.

The ascent complete, she strolled past the glitter of La Jolla's exclusive shops, closed for the night but beckoning customers to return the next day and purchase designer cocktail dresses in jeweled fabrics, twenty-four-carat strands of gold, and feather-soft furs in browns, grays and purest white. Idly Stephanie wandered from one bright window to the next, her thoughts jumbled. Christmas loomed three weeks away, and she yearned for the special warmth the season usually brought her.

Desperately she tried to absorb the spirit of the holiday decorations in the elegant shop windows. It was no use. Christmas held no promise this year. Upon hearing that a man was replacing Valerie as co-owner of the mingle, her parents had invented an immediate excuse for not coming to California this December. With her finances so tight, she could not afford to go home, and even if she could afford it, the disapproval of her parents removed all desire to spend the holidays in Indiana. She was curious to know if Lloyd had somewhere to celebrate the season, or someone to celebrate with. The questions made her aware again of how little she knew about this man who had become so involved in her life.

How naive she had been, to think she could agree to this joint purchase without any strings attached! The tension was building, ticking away like a time bomb. She wondered whether she could disarm it in time.

The streets emptied and her heated body cooled. She shivered in the chill ocean breeze, which swept in the first wisps of fog like puffs of dust from under a bed. Dust can't collect under water beds, she mused, then cursed herself for thinking of that undulating expanse of black.

Try as she might, she could not push away the fantasy of passion-filled hours with Lloyd, rocked by the liquid rhythm of the water bed. Her face burned with shame even as her body warmed with a different emotion. Damn it! Once again, she was physically attracted to a man who wanted everything from her, and promised nothing!

She tried to remember her plan of action formed this morning in the shower. She would begin seeing more of Jeremy. Perhaps it was unfair to Jeremy—no, she knew it was, but her back was against the wall and she could find no other way out for the time being.

She'd also start letting Sigmund out of his cage, taking him with her into the living areas she shared with Lloyd. Knowing how he felt about the bird, turning Sigmund loose sounded like teasing the lion at the zoo, but she would risk it. The danger of ending up in Lloyd's bed had become too great for her to take small precautions against it. She needed to be bold in her efforts.

The fog created halos around the streetlamps, and Stephanie hugged herself as the damp cold penetrated easily through the thin silk blouse. She surveyed the collection of restaurants in her imme-diate view, unable to work up any enthusiasm for entering one. Her inner turmoil deprived her of all inclination to eat. What she wanted, she knew, was a hot shower and a warm bed, but to get those she had to face Lloyd again. He'd probably time her damn shower!

She sighed, aware that many more minutes spent in the damp fog without a jacket would lead to a nasty cold. Her constant exposure to the ailments of her students made her an easy target if she al-lowed her resistance to lower. Common sense fi-nally took over, and she ordered her feet to take her back down the hill.

The cardboard sign propped in the drugstore window read OPEN, and on impulse she pushed through the swinging door and located the gay wrappers on the candy counter.

"Something for your sweet tooth, eh?" smiled the clerk as she paid for several packages of M & M Peanuts.

"You're not going to believe this, but the one who will eat these hasn't any teeth at all," she grinned in response.

"Really? Then I'd advise getting the regular kind. Those peanuts will give them trouble," the clerk said solemnly, as if filling a prescription.

Stephanie chuckled. "I don't think so. I'm buying them for my macaw, Sigmund."

"No kidding?" The little man exclaimed, eyebrows lifting. "It likes candy?"

"Not just any candy," she explained. "Only M & M Peanuts." She shrugged. "I'm not sure how good they are for him, but he's been eating them for five years, and it hasn't killed him yet."

"Those are expensive birds, aren't they?" The drugstore was empty, and Stephanie sensed the man's garrulous comments sprang from loneliness and boredom, but his friendly interest made her feel better.

"Yes, but fortunately I got Sigmund as a gift."

"Really? Does he talk?"

"I'm afraid so." Stephanie smiled ruefully, remembering how Sigmund's gift for gab had interrupted Lloyd's passionate lovemaking. And she was grateful, wasn't she?

"Boy, I'd love to have one of those birds, but I guess I'd rather buy a new car, instead. Besides, at my age, that kind of bird would outlive me, wouldn't it? I've heard they last as long as people do."

"So I'm told," Stephanie nodded. "It's an eerie feeling, isn't it, when you realize you have a pet for life?'' She had never considered Sigmund in that light before, but since she couldn't bear to give him away, anyone who chose to share her life would also be spending it with Sigmund. That certainly eliminated Lloyd. The thought brought her up short. She must really be off balance, entertaining ideas like that. She was trying to open her own clinic, not find a husband!

''Well, I hope Sigmund enjoys these,'' concluded the clerk, handing her the brown paper sack as another customer approached the register with a bottle of cough syrup. ''Nice talking to you.''

''Thank you,'' Stephanie answered warmly, glad to have the edge taken off her ill humor. Humming the latest country-music hit, she left the fluorescent brilliance of the drugstore and began the cold walk home, rehearsing what she would say to Lloyd when she arrived.

As it turned out, her rehearsal proved unnecessary, because Lloyd's door was closed when she walked into the apartment. There were no signs of his presence, although the faint smell of cooked hamburger told her he had eaten supper. The kitchen light was still on, almost as if he left it for her so she would not stumble around in the dark. Not willing to believe the action was motivated by consideration, she decided he just forgot to turn it off. Flipping the switch, she carried her bag of candy into the bedroom and quietly shut her own door, looking forward to a shower, a comfortable bed and a few of Sigmund's M & M candies.

"OKAY, SIGMUND, hop onto my shoulder," Stephanie coaxed several days later as she considered what to have for supper. From the doorway of her bedroom she could see Lloyd, sprawled in his shiny black chair reading a new scuba magazine. He shifted his large frame several times as she watched, and she enjoyed a secret smile of satisfaction. That darn chair wasn't even comfortable.

"Supper," croaked Sigmund, fluttering gently onto the towel she draped over one shoulder to protect her winter-white eyelet dress. One powerful talon hooked through the delicate material of the long-sleeved dress would ruin one of her favorite outfits. Under other circumstances she'd never allow him near the dress, but Sigmund had become her watchdog in the past few days. With him on her shoulder, Lloyd kept his distance, just as she planned.

"Come on, you crazy bird. I think you'll like the navel oranges I picked up today," she said as she left the sanctuary of her bedroom.

Lloyd's topaz eyes lifted from the pages of the magazine. "Yo, ho, ho and a bottle of rum."

"Trim the mainsail and lower the jib. We're in for a squall," she retorted, accustomed to his caustic remarks about Sigmund.

Lloyd snorted in amusement. "Do you even know what you're talking about?"

"Sort of. I've read *Treasure Island* and *Moby Dick*."

"And on the basis of that, I suppose you'd feel

competent to sail a square rigger out of San Diego harbor." He shook his head, chuckling.

"I assume among your many talents you know all about sailing boats, too?" She took a large orange from the refrigerator and began peeling it for Sigmund.

"Some," he admitted, folding the corner of the page he was reading and closing the magazine. "Anything to do with the ocean fascinates me. I love to be on the surface in a boat or under the surface in scuba gear. A lifetime isn't long enough to learn all there is to know about the ocean."

Sigmund sidled restlessly across Stephanie's shoulder, and she realized she'd stopped peeling the orange. "You really do love it, don't you?" she said, forcing herself back to the task of preparing food. "Most of my life I've been a confirmed land-lubber. My first glimpse of the ocean six years ago took my breath away, and I'm still getting used to the immensity of it. I swim in it now, but the idea of sailing or scuba diving is too advanced for me."

"Why? I'd be glad to teach you anything I could. It's a whole new world you're missing, Stephanie."

It was a generous offer, and she studied him for several moments, savoring the possibility, knowing she must refuse. "Thanks, but I don't think so."

"Okay." He picked up his magazine and resumed reading, but not before Stephanie caught the hurt in his eyes.

Casually he flipped the page, and she wondered if he was absorbing the words in front of him, despite his air of intense concentration. One hand came up to massage the back of his neck, and a sweet yearning rose in her to go to him and ease the strain in those broad shoulders.

As if sensing her focus of attention, he looked up. "You know, that dress makes you look like a sacrificial virgin."

"Is that your way of saying you don't care for it?" She was crushed. She always thought the dress complimented her blond hair and blue eyes.

"No, that's my way of saying I find it difficult to think of anything but making love to you."

The sweet yearning was rapidly displaced by a hot flame deep within her.

"So! We're back to that, are we?" Her fingers shook as she sectioned the orange and began feeding it to Sigmund.

"We never left it, Stephanie. You may think your little ploy of keeping Sigmund around will separate us, but it can't work forever. That bird is getting more used to me every day, and soon it won't matter whether he's in the room or not."

"If you imagine I need Sigmund to keep you at arm's length, you underestimate me, Lloyd," she hedged, grateful that Jeremy was arriving in a few minutes. "Now if you'll excuse me, I need to heat up this casserole and eat before Jeremy gets here."

"Ah yes, Jeremy. The other decoy. What have you cooked up to bring him on the scene this time?"

He knows. He knows what I'm doing, she thought frantically. But she'd play out the hand, anyway.

"I didn't 'cook up' anything. We're coleaders of a group therapy session tonight."

"In that dress? I thought group therapy involved punching pillows and venting your anger."

"It's obvious you have lots to learn about psychology," she said icily, stirring the hamburger and noodles as the cheese sauce bubbled in the pan.

"I learned everything I needed to learn when Jewel and I went through marriage counseling. God, but it was pointless!"

"You may have gotten a poor counselor. It happens." She spooned the hot casserole on a plate.

"This one seemed to have trouble with the English language. I told him repeatedly that I didn't love my wife, but he refused to accept it. Eventually I stopped trying to convince him."

"How could you be so certain you didn't love her?"

"I was sure." His tone was cold.

"But love is such a difficult term, Lloyd. Perhaps you—"

"Stephanie." His voice held her tightly from across the room. "Will you stop being a psychologist for this once, and answer me as a woman?"

Unwillingly she met his burning gaze. "All right."

"Would you know whether or not you loved someone?"

Why did the question have such an effect on her? Why was she shaking under the influence of his compelling eyes? Sexual attraction she would admit to, but love?

"Would you know, Stephanie?" he persisted,

and she noticed his own uneven breathing under his white dress shirt.

She took a deep breath. "Yes, I suppose I would."

"Good." He picked up his magazine once again. "I rest my case."

Stephanie stared down at her plate for several long moments, then picked it up and scraped the contents into the garbage. Jeremy had better arrive soon.

Just as she returned Sigmund to his cage, the doorbell rang. She fastened the stainless-steel latch and started out of the room when she remembered she'd need a sweater. By the time she took it from its hanger in the closet, she heard male voices. Lloyd had answered the door.

"Well, I see you two decided where to put the furniture," she heard Jeremy comment just before she walked into the room. She paused to hear Lloyd's response.

"It wasn't hard," Lloyd drawled. "All we had to do was call in some negotiators from the United Nations. I was awarded the left side of the living room and Stephanie occupies the right. The kitchen is the demilitarized zone."

"The combination of styles is...interesting." Jeremy, whose back was to her, leaned an elbow on the kitchen counter and propped his chin in his hand. "Maybe it will be a trend setter."

"Shouldn't we be going?" Stephanie said a little too loudly as she entered the room.

"You bet." Appreciation shone in Jeremy's pale eyes. "But I think I'd like to forget about the therapy session. That's one terrific dress."

"I'm afraid the outfit is my fault," Lloyd interjected. "She knew how much I've been wanting to see her in it. Thanks, Stephanie. It is lovely on you."

"You're welcome," she replied through clenched teeth. "After tonight I plan to burn it."

"Oh? I thought you weren't into burning articles of clothing?" Lloyd's eyes danced.

"At this moment all forms of arson sound appealing," she returned, smiling sweetly. "Shall we go, Jeremy?"

"By all means." He hurried toward the door, then held it for her.

"Bye, kids. Don't stay out too late," Lloyd called as she scurried into the night air.

Jeremy tucked his arm around her waist as they walked down the back stairs to the parking lot. "Alone at last," he sighed. "That Barclay fellow is giving you a rough time, isn't he?"

"It's not the easiest situation I've ever found myself in," agreed Stephanie, wishing she knew how to tactfully disengage Jeremy's arm. She wished she didn't feel as if she had just walked out the door with the wrong man. Lloyd was arrogant, overbearing and obnoxious. And vulnerable and funny, and sexier than any man she'd ever known, whispered an inner voice.

DESPITE HIS THREAT to circumvent her evasive tactics, Lloyd avoided Stephanie for the next few days. The majority of her classes fell during the morning hours, and he scheduled his lab work for after-

noons. Although she told herself she was de-
lighted, Stephanie found the hours she spent alone
in the apartment long and tedious.

As she drove home from the last day of class before Christmas vacation, she wished herself past
the upcoming two weeks. The jubilant energy of
her students distracted her from her own problems,
and her classes had become the most pleasant part
of her day. They were over until January, and all
she had to occupy her were the term papers stacked
beside her on the car seat.

The morning's heavy bank of fog refused to lift,
and random drops of water splashed against her
windshield as she pulled into her parking space. As
she expected, the black motorcycle was gone. She
could spend the afternoon with her term papers.
She grimaced, hurrying to cart them inside before
the rain started in earnest.

After fixing a peanut-butter sandwich for herself
and checking Sigmund's seed and water dishes, she
changed into her most comfortable jeans and a
pink oxford-cloth shirt, and settled into her rocker
with the first term paper. She plowed through
three of them before lifting her eyes with a sigh to
gaze at the dripping gray sky. The fog curtained off
everything except a barely visible line of ivory surf,
and even the dauntless gulls had lost all enthusiasm for the day. At least they have each other, she
thought, peering at the gray-and-white forms huddled together on the soft grass of the park.

The peal of her doorbell promised a reprieve
from her gloomy thoughts, and she decided even a

door-to-door salesman would get a friendly welcome from her this afternoon.

"This is the perfect day to curl up with a gorgeous blonde in front of a blazing fire. Look what I brought you." Proudly Jeremy produced two pressed-wood logs wrapped in red-and-black paper. "They even flame in colors. Shall we see if they work?"

"Why not?" Stephanie smiled gratefully into his round face, framed by damp tendrils of fine hair. "To tell you the truth, I don't know how well the fireplace draws."

"You've never used it?" He followed her happily into the living room, just like a puppy, she noticed, then chastised herself for being uncharitable. His happy-go-lucky personality was just what she needed.

"No. It just never seemed like the right time." She shrugged resignedly, and he nodded in understanding.

"You're still not getting along very well with Barclay, are you?" His tone reflected sympathy, but she read satisfaction in it as well.

"Not really," she admitted, wondering if he would make the connection between that statement and her sudden willingness to be in his company the past two weeks. They had seen a lot of each other, although she continued to refuse his sexual advances. This was the first time, however, that he had come to spend time with her in the apartment, and she realized it had never occurred to her to invite him, as if his presence would be a kind of intrusion. It felt a little that way at the moment, even though Lloyd would be gone all afternoon and need never know Jeremy had been there.

"Well, so much for that subject. I presume he's not here?" Jeremy set the logs on the circle of slate under the fireplace.

"No, he usually works in the lab during the afternoon."

"Good." Jeremy rubbed his hands together briskly. "Have you got some newspaper and matches?"

After incinerating several sections of newspaper and a book of matches, they finally coaxed a flame from one of the two logs.

"It's not exactly what I'd call blazing, but you are certainly gorgeous, so let's sit down and make the best of it," Jeremy said, pulling her next to him on the beige carpet.

"Shall I get the marshmallows?" she laughed, a little worried about what Jeremy had in mind. "Or how about popcorn? We could—"

"Stephanie, for God's sake. I'm not going to molest you, so sit here and be quiet."

The words sounded genuine enough, but Stephanie detected a gleam in his pale blue eyes when they traveled from her face to the smooth skin visible above her carelessly buttoned shirt. She wished she had fastened another button, knowing Jeremy could probably see the front clasp of her bra from his vantage point slightly above her. After a year of fending him off, she understood what a tiny suggestion of sexuality on her part did to his intentions, even if they had originally been honorable.

Deftly Jeremy slid his hand down her wrist, twining his fleshy fingers through hers. How soft his hands seemed compared to Lloyd's. Instantly she regretted the mental comparison, which brought a flood of memories and a pink tinge to her cheeks. The flush did not go unnoticed by Jeremy, who assumed he was having the desired effect on the woman seated beside him.

"What has Marge said lately about selling the place?" he asked, guessing the one topic that would keep Stephanie's interest as he casually released her hand and eased his arm around her shoulders.

"She thinks I can put it on the market in about six months," Stephanie answered, uncomfortably aware of the weight of Jeremy's arm. "I've been checking the paper for potential clinic sites, even though it's too early, and I've found several possibilities."

She began to forget Jeremy's arm around her as she warmed to her subject. "One sounded just perfect—not too far from the university, with an outer office and two private consulting rooms, and the rent wasn't bad. Depending on how much I can get out of my half of the mingle, I could supplement my income from clients and give myself several months to build up the practice until it pays for itself." Her sea-blue eyes sparkled with enthusiasm as she dreamed of the day when she could be her own boss.

"Don't forget I'll be helping you pay that rent," reminded Jeremy, using the opportunity to squeeze her more tightly to him. "My stocks just went up yesterday."

"That's good." Suddenly the air went out of her balloon of happiness. When she pictured the office space with two consulting rooms, she had trouble imagining Jeremy using one of them. Yet of course he would have to, because her plan would be difficult enough to implement even with financial help from Jeremy. She could never hope to do it alone. A soft sigh escaped her.

"Don't be discouraged, sweet Stephanie," Jeremy cajoled, his lips just inches from her ear. "The time will pass sooner than you think. By this summer, we'll be setting up that clinic together, and then, perhaps—" He left his sentence unfinished, but she had little trouble filling in the rest as he began to nibble past her shirt collar to the sensitive hollow of her throat.

"Jeremy," she pleaded, reaching to intercept his other hand, which was creeping across her thigh.

"Come on, Steph," he murmured against her skin, capturing her hand and holding it down by her side. "When I first saw you with that Barclay character I thought I'd lost out, but since you're not in tight with him, I'm restaking my claim."

His lips moved deliberately toward the creamy mound of her breast, pushing aside the pink material of her shirt. She tried to twist away from him, but he proved stronger than she thought, and her movement only pulled another button loose on her shirt.

"Let me go, Jeremy," she gritted between clenched teeth.

"Hey, we are long overdue for some of this." His wet lips felt hot against her skin.

"No, Jeremy." She pushed against him, but he clung to her stubbornly. A tiny surge of fear sang through her.

"Listen, Stephanie. We've known each other almost a year. How long d'you 'spect me to wait?" Jeremy's voice slurred with passion as he began tugging at the snap of her jeans.

"You don't understand. I don't want—" She tried to pry his fingers away. This was ridiculous! "If you'll just stop—" The resounding slam of a door accomplished her goal as Jeremy stiffened apprehensively. Lloyd! Lloyd was home!

"Sorry to have interrupted." His voice coiled like a steel spring. "I won't bother you."

The shock of the intrusion brought Jeremy's head up for an instant, and Stephanie grabbed her opportunity. "Lloyd!" The strangled cry halted his retreating footsteps.

"What?" She could feel his puzzled impatience.

"What do you want to talk to him for?" Jeremy laughed nervously and released her.

"I, um, didn't expect you back," Stephanie mumbled, buttoning her blouse and getting unsteadily to her feet.

"So I see." He turned toward his room. "I'll be going out again in a minute."

"No!" Stephanie started toward him and he turned, surprised. "I mean, Jeremy was just going."

"But—" Jeremy scrambled from the floor, adjusting his belt "—I thought you and I could—"

"You'd better leave, Jeremy. Now." Stephanie's eyes flashed a warning, and a new awareness brightened Lloyd's gaze.

"But, Stephanie," Jeremy pleaded.

"Go, Jeremy, before I say something we may both regret."

"Hey, if that's the way it is, fine with me." Jeremy edged toward the door, giving Lloyd a conspiratorial glance. "Never can tell about these females, can you? One minute they're ripping your clothes off, the next, they play the role of the soiled virgin."

"Your clothes look intact to me." Lloyd's jaw clenched. "Now I think you'd better go."

"Sure, sure." Jeremy backed toward the door, fumbling for the knob. "Maybe you'll have better luck than I did, pal." His eyes narrowed bitterly as he turned to Stephanie. "Give me a call when you get your head on straight." Then he was gone.

"Just what was going on here, Stephanie?" Concern and anger battled for dominance in the finely chiseled face.

Suddenly exhausted, Stephanie sank into the smooth coolness of her pine rocker. "He came over with some pressed-wood logs so we could have a fire. Then he just...got carried away...." Her voice trailed into a whisper as she felt the beginning surge of tears. She bowed her head, not wanting Lloyd to see them.

"Did he hurt you?" In an instant he was beside her, crouching next to the rocker. "Stephanie?"

"No," she murmured. "Oh, Lloyd, it was probably all my fault! I've been seeing more of him, and he just naturally thought that—"

"That he could force himself on you?" Lloyd grabbed her shoulders. "Stephanie, no man has the right to do that, no matter what he thinks! I hope you never let that jerk in here again." His voice was tight with emotion.

Stephanie looked up in surprise, forgetting her watery eyes. "But we're supposed to be clinic partners. I see him on campus all the time. What am I supposed to do?"

"I suggest you make sure you're never alone with him," Lloyd said quietly. "Unless you want to be mauled again. What do you suppose would have happened if I hadn't come home?"

Stephanie shuddered, remembering the panic she had felt. Still, it was hard to believe that Jeremy would ever harm her. "I think he would have stopped, Lloyd. He's not such a terrible person, really."

"If he tries to overpower a woman, he doesn't rate very high in my book. But then, I guess he's your problem. You're the one who's supposed to be nearly engaged to the guy." He stood up. "I can't really figure it, Stephanie. You claim to be so involved with him, but you don't want him laying a hand on you. If you were my fiancée, I'd expect a little more than a good-night peck on the cheek."

The idea of an engagement to Lloyd Barclay sent

shivers down her spine, and she took refuge in sarcasm. "We'll never have a chance to test that one, will we? The only kind of engagement we could have would be a military engagement."

"For once you're correct, Stephanie." He shrugged out of his white lab coat and hooked it over his shoulder. "Marriage isn't one of my favorite institutions."

"So you're content with one casual affair after another, is that it?" Her heart ached with the knowledge that Lloyd rejected marriage so completely. If she had ever dreamed, in the smallest corner of her mind of a life with him, that dream was just shattered.

"You could put it that way, except for one thing." His eyes held her transfixed. "My affairs are never casual."

5

"HOW WONDERFUL FOR YOU," Stephanie snapped, looking away from his tawny gaze.

"It could be wonderful for both of us, if you'd relax and let it happen," he said softly.

"Wonderful for how long, Lloyd? Six months? What happens when the magic's gone, and we're left living together? What happens when I have to sell at a loss because I can't wait to get away from you, or you from me? Our situation now may not be great, but it's tolerable. I plan to keep it that way until I get what I want out of this place—enough money for my clinic."

He considered her for a moment, then raked the lock of dark hair back from his forehead. "Still on track, aren't you?"

"You bet."

"Then there's no point in asking you to go with me to a Christmas party, is there? That's why I came home early. Some people from Scripps are getting together tonight, and I thought you might like to go, but—" He hesitated.

For the briefest second she wavered, touched that he had come home especially to invite her.

But would accepting be tantamount to saying she would go to bed with him? She couldn't chance it.

"No thanks, Lloyd."

"Then I'd better get ready."

Stephanie sat very still in the rocker after he left. Was she a fool to reject what he offered? Every day her longing sharpened. Why not enjoy the moment, forget the problems looming on the horizon? Why balk at a wonderful fling?

Because you've fallen in love with him, her heart answered. *Because when the affair is over, and it will be sooner or later, your life will be in little pieces.*

"Dear God," she muttered, burying her face in her hands. "What do I do now?" Slowly she rocked back and forth, listening to the splash of his shower. She had to get out of here, at least until he was gone for the evening!

Hurrying to her room, she bundled up in her forest-green parka, secured the hood over her golden curls, and left the apartment. A cold damp breeze blew across the fur fringing her face as she headed for the park. Breathing the rain-soaked air in great gulps, she welcomed the pelting drops, deliberately ran through puddles and felt the water seep through her canvas running shoes. Plopping down on the seawall, she listened to the muttering waves playing hide and seek in the fog. Slowly the light faded from the winter sky.

Unconsciously she kept her ears tuned for the sound of Lloyd's motorcycle, and when she heard it disappear down the street like a hive of angry bees, she pushed her soggy feet back to the apartment. Jeremy's logs lay cold and lifeless in the fireplace, but she had no desire to start them flaming again.

Stripping to the skin in her bathroom, she stepped into the warmth of her second hot shower of the day and stood under the pulsing spray until she lost all track of time. Squabbling about the electric bill was the least of her worries, she thought morosely as she dried herself and threw on a robe. Several days before she'd given up on installing a second meter after discovering the cost of parts and labor.

A cup of steaming tomato soup and several chapters of a novel later, she dozed off in her bed. Sometime after that the sound of the key in the lock awakened her, and as she switched off the bedside lamp she had left burning, she glanced at the clock. Much later she still lay in the dark, wide awake from imagining what he might have been doing until two o'clock in the morning.

"HOW ABOUT IT, Sigmund? Will you dress up and play Santa Claus this year?" Stephanie slumped dejectedly in her rocker the next evening, convinced this would be the worst Christmas of her life.

Every few minutes, prompted by a throaty gurgle from Sigmund, she reached into the glossy yellow bag in her hand and extracted two M & M Peanuts, one for her and one for her rainbow-hued companion. He clung precariously to the arm of the rocker, flapping his wings and gripping the curved wood with his beak when Stephanie shifted her weight and set the chair in motion.

"Sorry about that," she apologized to the bird. "I'll try not to rock your boat." *While mine is sinking*, she thought in despair.

She spent the day with her term papers, determined to blot out the disasters of the day before. When the entire stack was graded, she had nothing to erect between herself and her morbid thoughts. She could no longer consider Jeremy as a business partner for her clinic, which left no one to help her. Without a partner, it would take twice as much in savings before she could begin the project, which meant living in this mingle and building up equity for twice as long. She groaned aloud. She was having more trouble holding out against her attraction to Lloyd every day. The longer she stayed there, the better the odds that she would end up in his bed.

"Sigmund, the mind is willing, but the flesh is getting weaker by the minute," she said, stroking the bird's brilliant feathers.

"Pretty Stephanie," croaked Sigmund in response, nibbling gently on her finger. Stephanie still wondered if Lloyd had taught him the phrase, but she was glad for a kind word, even from her pet.

After all, she was dressed up a little. When the final paper was marked, she had rewarded herself with a long hot shower, again defiantly ignoring Lloyd's dictum. Perhaps because of the party she had missed the previous night, she decided to put

on a scarlet lounging outfit. The harem pants and
scoop-necked top with dolman sleeves gave her a
festive look she was far from feeling, but she might
as well look good on the outside, she reasoned,
strapping on gold sandals and a delicate three-
strand gold necklace.

She had bought the lounge wear several months
before during a shopping trip with Valerie, who
had encouraged her to get "something sufficiently
flamboyant to complement that wild-looking bird
you own." Well, there she was, all decked out with
her red outfit and her red-, yellow- and blue-
feathered friend, and no one around to appreciate
the show. Feeling very sorry for herself, she decided to pour a glass of Jeremy's white wine, which
she had been hoarding in the refrigerator for a special occasion.

"This may be as special as it gets, Sigmund," she
sighed as she unscrewed the cap from the bottle
and splashed a little of the silvery liquid in a goblet.
"If only he weren't so damned attractive," she continued, pretending for a moment the bird could
understand her. "And those tawny eyes drive me
crazy!"

"Those tawny eyes!" echoed Sigmund with the
proper dose of reverence in his gravelly voice.

"Uh, oh. Better watch who you repeat that little
phrase to, my friend, or my subterfuge may be
over." She took a mouthful of wine from her too-
full glass and allowed its cool bite to slide across
her tongue before she recrossed the room to sink
into her rocker once more. Between sips she contin-

ued to feed Sigmund M & M candies as she reviewed her impossible situation. She was in love with the man she lived with, yet unable to act or speak as if she cared at all.

With a sigh she drained the last of her wine and pondered the advisability of having a second glass on an empty stomach. She sat debating the point when suddenly the door swung open and the pungent scent of pine needles filled the room.

"Ho, ho, ho. Merry Christmas!"

Stephanie peered through the mass of branches being stuffed energetically through the door and watched in fascination as Lloyd continued in a jovial bass, "Have you been a good little girl this year?"

Totally disarmed, she fell in with his game. "I'm afraid not, Santa," she answered in a tiny falsetto. "But I'm a world-champion tree trimmer, so maybe I can make up for my misdeeds."

"How can you be the world-champion tree trimmer?" questioned Lloyd in his normal voice as he managed to shove the tree all the way through the door in a shower of needles. "I am the world-champion tree trimmer."

"Correction. You may hold the title in the men's division, but I'm the champion in the women's division. This has never been, in the history of the sport, a coed contest." Stephanie grinned up at him, sniffing appreciatively the combination of cold and pine scent on his corduroy jacket. She couldn't see any harm in trimming a tree together. Her eyes lingered on his dark hair tousled by the wind, and his cheeks flushed by the effort of wrestling the seven-foot tree up to the apartment. He looked wonderful.

"Damn! And all this time that's what I had in mind. Could we consider changing the rules for this year?" His golden eyes sparkled in fun, and she realized she had never seen him like this.

"I'll take it up with the commissioner. What do you say, Mr. Freud?" She turned to Sigmund, who had been eyeing the large pine with a mixture of curiosity and suspicion.

"Pretty Stephanie," he squawked, shifting from one taloned foot to another.

"The commissioner has agreed to a rule change, as long as it doesn't set a precedent," Stephanie said solemnly, hoping Lloyd would not believe she had taught her own bird to pay her compliments.

"Thank you, Mr. Commissioner." Lloyd bowed in Sigmund's direction while maintaining his hold on the tree.

"Those tawny eyes!" croaked Sigmund, enjoying the attention he was getting and trying to prolong it.

"What did he say?" Lloyd glanced questioningly at Stephanie, who was busy studying the ceiling.

"Oh, some nonsense, I expect," she said as casually as she could manage, not daring to look at him. Darn that bird's loose beak!

"If you say so." Amusement lurked at the corners of his mouth, but he did not challenge her evasion. "By the way, you look like you were expecting a tree-trimming contest." An assessing gaze took in her gaily colored outfit, lingering on the low-scooped neckline accented with the triple strand of fine gold. "Very nice, Stephanie."

"Thank you." Why was she blushing like one of her freshman students? Men had noticed her appearance before. Embarrassed, she changed the subject. "That's a nicely shaped tree, but I hope it isn't getting resin on the carpet."

"Oops!" Hastily he picked the trunk off the floor, running his fingers over the cut edge. "It doesn't seem to be oozing. Probably because it's been cut so long. With only two days until Christmas, the lot was practically giving them away." He grinned sheepishly. "I never could resist a bargain."

Which is why we're standing here today, thought Stephanie. "It's very beautiful," she said aloud, "but I'm fresh out of Christmas-tree stands. How are we going to put it up?"

"Fear not. Would the world-champion tree trimmer—of the men's division—arrive without the proper equipment? We'll just lean the tree against the counter for now."

He laid down the pine gently, but as he released the trunk, the tree slid sideways toward the floor and Stephanie rushed forward to stop it from falling. Their fingers grasped the rough bark at the same instant, and as their hands touched, Stephanie felt a jolt of electricity travel up her arm. She jerked away her hand as he slowly righted the tree, his eyes never leaving hers.

"I'll be right back," he said softly, and she nodded, not trusting herself to speak. Lloyd had cast a powerful spell over her. Even a chance touch could turn her into a basket case! He bounded out the door, and during the few minutes he was gone, a hundred questions occurred to her. Why had he bought the tree? Had he purposely intended to share it with her, or was it only because she happened to be home when he arrived?

Frantically she tried to summon her resolve of the afternoon before, but somehow, standing there in her red outfit looking at the Christmas tree he had bought—*their* Christmas tree—she could only feel a happy warmth building inside her. Maybe she was finally getting the Christmas spirit. Perhaps that was all it was. *Sure. Don't kid yourself,* whispered the little voice in the back of her mind.

"I think I thought of everything," Lloyd announced as he strode back in the room with a large sack and a trussed-up bundle of firewood.

"How did you transport all that stuff on your motorcycle?" she gasped in amazement.

"The bag and the wood I tied in the passenger seat, and I strapped the tree across the bike from front to back. I felt a little like one of King Arthur's knights on my trusty black steed, as a matter of fact." He grinned. "Got any dragons you need slain, m'lady?"

Stephanie shook her head. "It's been a poor year for dragons. But I do have some wassail for m'lord's pleasure, after we finish trimming the tree." She nodded toward her empty glass next to the rocker.

"Then let's get to it!" Lloyd deposited the bag

on the floor and carried the bundle of wood to the hearth. "But first we'll start a fire," he added, peeling off his corduroy coat and squatting before the conical firebox. Opening the screen, he surveyed the half-burned commercial logs on the grate. "Never did like these darn things," he mumbled, blackening his hands as he pulled out the pieces and set them on the far side of the hearth. Quickly he untied his bundle of wood, located some newspaper, and within minutes had created a cheerful blaze. "There. We should have done that a long time ago," he said, satisfaction evident in his voice.

Stephanie watched the warm light of the fire ease the lines from his face and felt a rush of protectiveness. She realized that her need to give, to share, was absorbing all her caution. It would be so easy to cross the short distance between them, allow her fingers to work the tension out of the broad shoulders hunched by the flickering logs, but she held back. Was Lloyd capable of returning her love with the kind of total commitment she needed to survive? She needed time...time to find out.

"Christmas carols!" Lloyd said suddenly, snapping his fingers and jumping to his feet. "I'm almost sure I have a tape of Christmas carols." He turned toward her with a worried expression. "You do like Christmas music?"

"My favorite kind," she chuckled, thinking how like a little boy he looked.

"Good." He disappeared into his bedroom, returning with a cassette player and one tape. Soon

Bing Crosby's "White Christmas" chased the last bit of gloom from the apartment, and Stephanie hummed along, anticipating—what? She focused on the tree, trying not to think.

"Now let's get the ground rules for this trimming contest straight." Lloyd sat on the floor assembling the metal tree stand. "Would you please bring the tree over, Stephanie?"

She lifted the fragrant pine and eased it through the ring at the top of the stand, acutely aware of Lloyd's head only inches from her thigh. He cleared a telltale hoarseness from his throat. "Okay. Lights are a combined effort, but after that each of us gets half the decorations and half the tree, and Sigmund will judge the results. Fair enough?"

"Sounds fair," nodded Stephanie gravely. "And icicles go on one strand at a time, right?"

"That's the only way to do it," he agreed with equal seriousness.

As they worked to unwind the two strands of lights, Stephanie caught a flurry of red, blue and gold wings from the corner of her eye. "Sigmund!" she cried in sudden apprehension, dropping the lights to the floor, but it was too late. The large bird circled the tree once, then landed on the topmost branches like a giant decoration. Had the tree been rooted in the forest, it might have held him, but the flimsy metal stand offered little support for the weight of a forty-inch macaw. The tree toppled as an indignant Sigmund flew screeching back to his perch on the rocking chair. Cold hands gripped Stephanie's heart as she rushed to right the tree, wondering if Sigmund had just ruined their Christmas mood.

"At least the stand didn't have water in it," chuckled Lloyd from beside her, and he stooped to check the screws anchoring the pine.

"Lloyd, I'm so sorry," she wailed, checking the tree for broken branches.

"I'd say that was a perfectly natural reaction on his part," said Lloyd, and Stephanie heard with surprise the friendly understanding in his voice. She thought he hated Sigmund! "Birds and trees go together, that's all. But maybe you'd better put him back in his cage for the time being, anyway."

"Of course." She coaxed Sigmund to her arm and retreated to the bedroom. "Lloyd, would you please bring that bag of M & M Peanuts?" she called as she struggled to make Sigmund accept forced confinement. No matter how many times she tried to get him through the door of his cage, he managed to hook his beak or a claw on the outside and circumvent going in.

"Why? You get a sudden candy attack?" asked Lloyd, walking into the room with the bag in his hand.

"It's for Sigmund," she explained, continuing to wrestle with the large bird. "If I put some in his cage, I may be able to get him in it."

"He likes these things?"

"Loves them. Just pour some in my hand." She reached one hand behind her and felt Lloyd take it in his own and drop several smooth candies into it. Quickly she withdrew from the warmth of his grasp as Sigmund watched her with bright yellow eyes. "Okay, Sigmund, this is a little bribe to get you in your cage. You know it and I know it, but it works, doesn't it?" She trickled the candies into his seed cup one at a time, making sure he heard them clink into the ceramic dish. Sigmund gave her one long look, then hopped to the floor of his cage and picked up a candy in his curved beak. Noiselessly Stephanie closed the cage door and stood up.

"I'll be damned," exclaimed Lloyd. "He does like them." He gazed down at Stephanie, indulgent amusement and something else—something that made her catch her breath—in his rugged face. "That's some bird you've got, lady."

"I care about him a lot," she confessed, wanting Lloyd to know how much Sigmund meant to her. Breathing became more and more difficult as her mind returned to the last time they had been in this room together.

"I know," whispered Lloyd, and he brushed her lips gently with his fingertips. She half closed her eyes, expecting his kiss, but it never came. "Let's go decorate the tree," he said, a suspicious catch in his voice.

Side by side they worked in a room lit only by the multicolored glow of the tree lights and the orange blaze of the fire. They played Lloyd's tape again, not minding the repetition of the familiar carols pouring from the tape player.

"I'm almost done," announced Stephanie, carefully draping another icicle over the tip of a feathery green branch. "Time counts, too, you know."

"It does?" Lloyd responded in mock anguish. "Then forget the rules!" He began flinging handfuls of icicles on his half of the tree.

"Stop! You can't do that!" Laughing, she rushed around the tree and caught his arm. "That looks terrible," she scolded, taking the icicles out of his grasp. "I think you just forfeited."

"What about the penalty you get for holding?" He looked significantly at her hand, and she dropped it from his arm, suddenly self-conscious.

"Um, I guess maybe the contest is a draw," she murmured, sneaking a look at his face through the fringe of her blond lashes.

"You're afraid to pay the penalty," he teased, his golden eyes sparkling.

"What is it?"

"Just a kiss," he said casually, but the husky timbre of his voice betrayed the emotion he tried to disguise.

"Oh, is that all?" She worked to remain as cool as he. She could play games, too. Standing on tiptoe, she pecked him on the cheek with pursed lips. "There. Penalty paid."

"Not quite," he said softly, his arms snaking around her. "After all, yours was a major infraction. The punishment must fit the crime," he murmured just before his lips crushed against hers and his arms tightened, bringing her hard against his lean body. His assault was quick, demanding, and just as quickly Stephanie felt the floodgates of her pent-up need burst open, filling her with molten desire. Her mouth opened fully before the onslaught of Lloyd's tongue, and she arched her quivering body against him as her arms wound around his waist, urging him closer.

With a groan muffled against her lips, Lloyd tangled his fingers in the mass of gold curls, cradling her head and deepening the kiss, exploring the moist softness of her mouth with his seeking tongue. A raging fire built within Stephanie's loins as she squirmed against him, wanting him, loving him, impatient at the fabric that separated their yearning bodies.

Gasping, Lloyd wrenched his mouth free and covered her face and throat with tiny nipping kisses. "You temptress," he rasped hoarsely. "That scarlet outfit has turned me into a raging bull—don't you know that? God, Stephanie, how I want you, have wanted you, ever since I first saw you standing there in that disreputable sweat shirt, belligerent as hell about the prospect of living with me."

"I was afraid, Lloyd," she murmured against his cheek. "I still am."

"Don't be. I won't hurt you." His breath was hot against the hollow of her throat, and his hands slipped up her bare back under the red top, undoing the catch of her bra.

"How can you be so sure?" she choked out, her body rebelling against any restraint; her mind wanting to believe she could trust him. She could not deny him what he wanted, what she wanted too, but she craved reassurance, even if later it proved false.

"Feel what's happening between us, Stephanie, and tell me that it's wrong."

"You know I can't say that."

"Then let it happen. How can something so right be bad for you? I can feel you trembling, Stephanie, and I know you want me, too." He placed his hand gently over her breast. "I can feel your heart racing out of control, just like mine." His fingers played tenderly with the hard peak of her nipple. "Tell me you want me, Stephanie." He smiled into her love-glazed eyes. "All I want for Christmas is to hear you say it."

"I want you, Lloyd," she whispered, "but—"

"No, no more words." He laid a finger lightly over her lips. "No more soul-searching, Stephanie. No promises, no commitments. Just tonight."

She swallowed, as if to rid herself of the words of love she had almost spoken. He was not ready to hear them, perhaps would not have believed they were true. *But I do love you*, she wanted to scream at him. *It's real*! But the words lodged in her throat as his mouth covered hers and he lowered her gently to the carpet. The Christmas-tree lights danced across the gold strands of her necklace as he unclasped it and laid it on the beige rug.

"I want you free of all adornment," he whispered. "Take out your earrings." Silently she obeyed, slipping the gold loops free and tossing them toward the necklace. Slowly he undressed her, pushing her scarlet top easily over her head and sliding her bra free, exposing the top half of her body to his burning gaze.

She expected him to touch her then, longed for him to caress her throbbing breasts, but he moved instead to one gold sandal, unbuckling it with care as she lay clenching her hands, the aching void building inside her. Lazily his tongue teased the arch of her foot, and she squirmed involuntarily.

"Ticklish?" he chuckled, removing her other shoe.

"Yes."

"Good." He moved up beside her and his fingers found the waistband of her harem pants. "That means all your nerve endings are in good working order. I'm going to make them sing tonight, lovely lady." Deftly he drew away her last bits of clothing and she lay before him in the soft light of the Christmas tree.

His sharp intake of breath was the only sound in the stillness as she watched his eyes move over her flushed skin. An eternity passed as she remained perfectly still, taut with leashed emotion. At last his fingertips began brushing slow circles along her arms, down her breasts, across her stomach, along her thighs, caressing her until she released her breath in ragged gasps.

"You were enchanting tonight in your scarlet and gold," he murmured, his voice rich with desire. "But this is how I've longed to see you."

She looked into his face, watching the leaping flames from the fire mirrored in eyes dark with passion. Carefully she traced the line of his mouth with one finger, smiling tremulously when he caught it between his teeth.

"Do you bite?"

"Oh, yes," he answered around the finger he held prisoner. "But not fingers." Freeing her, he bent his mouth to her breast, nipping playfully at the soft flesh, then taking the aroused nipple with an erotic pressure that brought a moan to Stephanie's lips. As he continued to tease the sensitive tip, his hand moved in ever-tightening circles toward the source of her pleasure, and she instinctively arched her hips in invitation.

"What do you want, Stephanie?" he smiled against her silken skin. "Show me."

Color surged into her cheeks as he raised his head to look directly into the blue depths of her eyes. "Show me, Stephanie," he repeated, his fingers drawing a tantalizing circle around her center of passion. Flushing still deeper, she took his hand in her own, guiding it to where the pulsing ache filled her, making her throw away any vestiges of shame.

"Yes," he whispered, his mouth covering hers as his hand sent waves of pleasure through her heated body. Groaning, she fumbled with the buttons of his shirt, impatient for all he had to offer her. "Easy, my little wildcat," he laughed. "I can't afford to have my clothes destroyed. Better let me do it this time. You can do it another time, when you are willing to be careful." He moved away from her slightly and stood up, and she felt a deep sense of loss.

"Lloyd, I want you so," she confessed, watching him slip out of his shirt and unhook the belt of his trousers.

"I know, but no more than I want you, my curly-headed moppet. How can someone look so innocent and so sexy at the same time?" He smiled down at her, unashamed as her eyes devoured the proud thrust of his chest sprinkled with dark hair, the tight muscles of his belly, and his jutting manhood, blatantly announcing his desire.

As he knelt beside her, she reached to stroke him. Relishing his soft moan of pleasure as he sank beside her, she let her hands roam at will, giving as good as she had gotten, making him shudder convulsively as she continued her loving ministrations.

"Can't take much more of that, Stephanie," he warned in a husky voice, rolling to face her. "Come here, moppet." Once again his hand found the core of her need for him and she arched against the welcome pressure, wanting more, wanting all of him.

"And I can't take much more of that," she gasped as his tongue flicked against the inside of her thigh, moving ever higher. When his tongue continued the probing rhythm of his fingers, she cried out, no longer in control of her voice, "Lloyd, please, now!"

"Yes, now," he murmured, his lips suddenly close to her ear as she felt his invasion and rose joyfully to meet it. After a few powerful strokes he paused, and she knew he was keeping iron control of himself, wanting to give to her as well. Moving under him, she grasped his firm buttocks and urged him on, aware her own explosive response was only seconds away. With a strangled cry, he plunged against her again and again, and she called to him as the pressure building within her finally burst, the sensation carrying her away just as he fell trembling against her, gasping her name.

6

STEPHANIE AWOKE to the clunk of wood against metal. Pushing back a furry blanket that had a vaguely familiar texture, she sat up and watched Lloyd, clad only in his pants, using one of the unburned logs to rearrange the dying coals in the fireplace.

"I feel like a cavewoman," she remarked to his naked back as she wrapped the soft blackness around her bare shoulders. "Do we need the fire to keep the saber-toothed tiger at bay?"

"I guess my thumping around woke you, huh?" He turned to grin at her, the errant lock of dark hair cutting a diagonal swath across his forehead. "The truth is, I wanted you to wake up."

"Oh?" She arched one brow and smiled suggestively.

"And not even for the reason you think, smarty." He gave up on the fire and came toward her on all fours. "Although that idea has merit, too. But I feel like getting some fresh air. Let's go for a walk along the cliffs."

"Now?" Stephanie peered into the darkness outside the sliding door. "It must be three o'clock in the morning."

"Two-thirty, to be exact. That makes it even better. Nobody else will be out there."

"Nobody but the muggers and rapists, that is."

"Nobody will bother us, Stephanie," he said patiently, and looking at his rock-hard muscles in the faint glow of the fire, she felt a little better.

"Are you a karate expert?" she asked hopefully.

"Judo. But I've never had to use it. Come on, let's get going before the moon sets!"

"Okay." Impulsively she jumped up, then blushed as she realized she had nothing on.

Lloyd's eyes burned like the embers in the fireplace. "On second thought, let's discuss our other option, now that you're awake."

"No, we're going for a walk," she said firmly, stepping away from his outstretched hand. "Before the moon sets. Then we'll see about that other option."

"Then get out of here and quit tantalizing me with that deliciously curved behind!" he growled playfully, and she scampered into her bedroom to don jeans and a warm flannel shirt, buttoning it over her bare breasts, enjoying the cotton softness against her tender nipples. The slight soreness brought back the feel of his even white teeth, and warmth radiated from the center of her body.

"No, we're going for a walk," she repeated to herself, wanting to experience every sensuous delight with Lloyd. But the walk was important. She welcomed a chance to learn more about the man she loved.

Hastily flicking a brush through her curls, Stephanie paused in midstroke, evaluating the sparkling eyes and rose-tinged cheeks of the woman in the bathroom mirror. She had capitulated to Lloyd's demands—and her own, she admitted—and she felt like a child at her first circus.

But Lloyd had not mentioned love. How far would the physical attraction he felt for her carry them? She had placed her own plans in jeopardy this evening, destroyed any hope of a purely business relationship. She was risking everything on the chance he might learn to love her as she loved him.

Soberly she stared into the blue eyes grown suddenly thoughtful. "Good luck, Stephanie Collier," she whispered.

Pulling on her green parka, she walked back to the living room where Lloyd stood, corduroy jacket in hand, admiring the tree. "Damn good job," he said in an official tone, circling the fragrant pine. "Professional job."

"I agree," Stephanie said, cocking her tousled head to one side. "But which side is more professional?"

"It's hard to say," he replied, moving around the tree to take her in his arms. "You see, I can't tell where one half stops and the other half begins."

"I know what you mean," she breathed before his mouth claimed hers in a gentle velvet touch. He released her and smiled into her eyes.

"Let's go for that walk," he said softly, and she nodded, anxious for the chance to know him better.

He held her hand, his fingers laced comfortably through hers as they scurried down the stairs, arriving breathless and laughing at the bottom of the four-flight trip. Running like children, they crossed the deserted street and the damp grass of the park before pausing at the low rock wall separating the park from the cliffs of the cove.

A half-circle moon hung on the horizon like a nickel stuck in a penny candy machine, its light paving a silver path across the dark water in front of them. Stephanie watched the path blur as the cresting waves smashed against the cliffs at their feet.

"It looks a little forbidding," she murmured, edging closer to Lloyd's comforting bulk.

"It can be very dangerous for those who get careless," Lloyd agreed, releasing her hand to pull her close beside him. "We're land animals, after all. The ocean is not our natural environment."

"It must be exciting to scuba dive."

"Yes." His voice surrounded her, rich and warm. "Penetrating into that forbidden world is a wonderful challenge, one I haven't been able to resist ever since I was a kid." He stared at the expanse of water, as if somehow he wanted to become one with it.

"Then you've always wanted to be a marine biologist?"

"I've always wanted to have some kind of career in oceanography, and that's the one I finally settled on."

She detected a catch, a hesitancy in his reply, but

she pushed on, wanting to know the details of a life that had led him to this point and to her. "So you got a scholarship after high school and went right through to your doctorate, never dissuaded from your goal, right?" She pictured a one-track approach to life, and wondered if she had guessed correctly.

"Not quite." His jaw tightened in the moonlight, and the warm weight of his arm dropped from her shoulder. "Let's walk," he said curtly, taking her hand almost casually in his own.

She had hit a sore point, she was certain. She hoped he would open up and tell her about it, trust her with the secrets in his life. His next question caught her completely by surprise, so far from her thoughts was its intent.

"I'm a little late in asking, but are you by any chance on the pill?"

"Y-yes, I am," she stammered, not liking the clinical sound of his voice.

"Thank God!"

His evident relief brought a pinprick of disappointment. He wanted no complications from her, that was obvious.

"I guess being a single woman in California, you would be," he continued, "but I shouldn't have taken it for granted."

"And just what does that mean? Are you implying that I sleep around?" The magic of the evening was quickly dissolving, being replaced with anger and hurt. "For your information, it makes my cycle easier to manage if I take them." No need to tell him about Gary, about Gary's demand that she get the prescription in the first place. After he'd left, she kept taking the pills out of habit, and it did make her cycle more predictable.

"You don't have to justify to me, Stephanie. I'm damn glad you're taking it, and I hope you didn't forget today."

"No, I didn't," she said miserably. A large wave hit the rocks below, sending moonlit drops like tears fountaining into the air.

"At least one of us was responsible, then." His words battered her heart. "I should have thought to take precautions myself, but I guess a fool never learns." His bitterness stopped her in midstride, and she whirled to face him.

"Aren't you being a little hard on yourself? It's not as if we planned this tonight." But did he? The moonlight splintered like glass as moisture pooled in her eyes. "Or was it planned, Lloyd?" she asked softly.

He touched her cheek, brushing away a single tear with his thumb. "Hey, I'm sorry, my little moppet," he said gently. "I guess I've been a little rough on you." He brought up his other hand to cup her face. "To answer your question, no I didn't really plan tonight, but—"

"But what, Lloyd?" She tried to still her quivering lip.

"But I'd be less than honest if I told you it was the furthest thing from my mind. When I passed the Christmas-tree lot on my way home tonight, I thought of you. Crazy, huh?"

"Not to me. I love Christmas trees."

Tenderly his thumbs traced and retraced her cheekbones, and she felt her anger ebb.

"Somehow I knew that, so I decided to get you one. I figured if you weren't home, I'd decorate it myself and surprise you. If you were, and I hoped fervently you would be, we'd decorate it together."

"And that's all?" she couldn't resist asking.

"Uh, not quite all."

"What else?" A smile worked its way to the edges of her mouth.

"After we finished the tree, I thought we could sit by the fire, enjoy the Christmas lights, and... talk." He assumed the innocent expression of a child who had just eaten the last cookie in the jar.

"Lloyd! You had a campaign all mapped out, didn't you?"

"Okay, I schemed a little, but what about your share of the blame? What about that red number you greeted me with, complete with gold jewelry and gold sandals, no less? If you want to keep me at a distance, I suggest a frowsy housecoat and moth-eaten slippers that go flop, flop when you walk."

"That's all that it takes to turn you off?" she laughed.

"It might have worked originally, but even that won't help now. Now I know what you'd be hiding under the housecoat." He leered and caught her to him, moving his hips deliberately against hers.

"Lloyd Barclay, we're in public!" she protested, pushing ineffectively against his chest.

"Public? Where?" Dutifully he scanned the park. "Nope. My public has disappeared."

"Except for me," Stephanie chuckled, snuggling against his chest. Her good mood was restored, but something Lloyd had said niggled at the back of her mind. Something about "a fool never learns." What had he meant? She hesitated, not wanting to destroy the peaceful silence. The question grew larger, and she couldn't hold it back.

"Lloyd...you said a little while ago that...that 'a fool never learns.'"

She felt him go still in her arms, knew when he lifted his head and stared out toward the rolling waves.

"It was a long time ago, Stephanie."

"But you haven't forgotten, have you?"

"No." He dropped his arms and turned away from her, facing the ocean.

"Please tell me, Lloyd." The request sounded too intense, and she bit her lip. Her psychologist's training worked just fine until she came up against her own problems. She should have adopted a well-modulated tone, a slightly disinterested "Would you like to talk about it?" She registered the belligerent set of his jaw and wondered if she'd blown it.

"All right." The line of his jaw eased, and his shoulders sagged a little. She felt his pain, but also something more important—trust. She sighed, knowing he was offering her a gift more precious than a lot full of Christmas trees.

His words came slowly at first, rough edged, as

he searched for a way to tell her a story that never
had been fully told.

"It was my senior year in high school. Jewel's
too. You've heard this part before—homecoming
queen and captain of the football team are a tradi-
tional pair. We were like two healthy young animals, experiencing physical love for the first time. I
had big plans for college, was saving money and
working for those scholarships you mentioned. I
told Jewel all that. I asked her to go on the pill, even
paid for the doctor visit and the prescription. She
even *showed* me the darn things!"

"But she didn't take them?"

"Not even one. She wanted to get married so bad
she didn't care if she tricked me into it. That's what
she told me after she announced she was pregnant."

"In this day and age, Lloyd, there are alternatives
to marriage in a case like this." She spoke gently,
sensing in advance what his response would be.

"Not for me. I was furious at first, wanted to kill
her, but then it dawned on me that she was carrying my child, as well as hers. I had to marry her,
had to protect this part of me she had growing inside her. I know it's medieval thinking, and I tried
to talk myself out of the sense of connection to that
life, but I couldn't. We got married in June."

"And the child?"

He laughed shortly. "That's the joke of it. She
miscarried in July. I should have filed for divorce
immediately, but she paraded her grief, wailed
constantly about the baby, and since I felt pretty

bad myself, I believed that she needed me to help her through that rough time. I stayed, kept my job as a low-level manager for a department store, and gave up plans to register for school in the fall. When the second semester came around, she seemed to be in better shape, so I announced I was leaving and going back to school. That's when she really turned on the waterworks, and even offered to go to work herself so I could take a full load of classes."

"Sounds pretty unselfish," Stephanie admitted, although she wanted to hate this woman.

"I thought so, too. I knew I didn't love her, but she seemed to love me enough for both of us, and she was so pitiful, sobbing her eyes out and begging me to stay. We had a long talk that night, and I told her that after I finished school I wanted to start a family. That near-taste of fatherhood had done something to me, and I wanted children. She agreed. She would have agreed to anything."

"Lloyd...." She touched his sleeve and felt him tremble. "Were there children?" She had to know.

"No." Her heart lurched at the regret in his voice, but a cool breeze of relief blew across her conscience. Children formed a bond between two people, and right now she did not want Lloyd bound to his ex-wife. "After I earned my doctorate, I kept bringing up the subject, but she always had a reason why we shouldn't begin yet. First we needed a house, then a swimming pool, then a new car. Finally she admitted the truth after she'd had one too many ounces of gin. She didn't want

babies, had never wanted them. Having babies ru-
ins a woman's figure, she said. The only reason she
tried to get pregnant the first time was to land me.
Now she figured she had me locked in with our
material possessions and our life-style. She vowed
she'd take me to the cleaners financially if I walked
out on her. I did, and she did, and the rest you
know." He kept his back to her.

"Lloyd, I'm so sorry." Stephanie slipped her
arms around his waist and laid her cheek against
the ribbed roughness of his jacket. For a moment
he stood stiffly, his arms at his sides. Stephanie
continued to hold him, pouring her love out silently . . . waiting.

Slowly the tension seeped out of him, and at last
he turned in her arms and reached to cup her face
in his hands. "I'm sorry, too, Stephanie. I let that
memory invade our happiness tonight." The tangy
salt breeze filled her nostrils and lifted the lock of
hair from his forehead. Joy surged through her at
the growing warmth in his golden eyes as he
studied her face, tracing the line of her freckles
across her upturned nose. "You look like a blond
version of Little Orphan Annie, did you know
that?" His soft smile made her heart ache.

"Why do you suppose I wear my hair like this?"
she teased, trying to keep her tone light.

"Well, I may not be Daddy Warbucks, but I'd like
to take you home," he whispered, planting light
kisses along the bridge of her nose.

"Convince me," she vamped, moistening her lips
suggestively.

With a throaty chuckle, he captured her smiling mouth with his own, and she answered with an explosion of passion that startled her. She pressed every available inch of her small frame along his body, moving sensuously against him until he moaned in protest. "Slow down a little, huh?" he laughed against her cheek. "How can I take you home with me if I can't even walk?"

She could feel the swell of his manhood against her hip, and realized the truth of his statement. Smiling provocatively, she backed away. "Ah, but can you run?" she taunted, then spun in the wet grass and sprinted toward the lamplit street. She heard his rapid footsteps behind her and ran faster, crossing the damp asphalt before a strong hand reached around her waist and she was pulled, giggling, into his barely heaving chest.

"You're...you're not even winded!" she panted.

"Comes from good clean living." He grinned down at her. "Now let's get inside before you get me arrested. Did it ever occur to you how that little scene might look to a policeman?"

"No." She lowered her eyes in chagrin. When she raised them again, mischief winked in their blue depths. "But I'd visit you in jail."

"Upstairs, you wench!" He slapped her roundly on the seat of her worn jeans and she bounded ahead of him, keenly aware of the exact level of his gaze as he followed her.

The Christmas tree filled the room with its forest scent, and Stephanie breathed deeply as she walked past the door Lloyd swung open for her. The colored lights perched on the dark branches like gum-drops, and the breeze from the open door shivered the icicles cascading in twinkling profusion from Lloyd's side and in delicate filigree from hers.

"I can certainly tell which side of the tree you *threw* your icicles on," she commented dryly.

"Christmas is the season for abundance, didn't you know?" he retorted.

"But in the case of icicles, less is more." She reached to remove a clump of tangled silver. "Now you have to admit this is ridiculous," she accused, extending the shiny mass toward him. "What's so funny?" He stood watching her, hands on hips, his face creased in a deep grin.

"This is the same argument my mother and dad had every year. I just realized how much fun they were having all that time."

Stephanie smiled, too, then sobered. "You did say 'had,' not 'have'?"

"Yeah, I'm afraid so. Dad died of a heart attack. Mom lasted about two years after that, but she was never the same. They never did find out what was wrong with her, but that's because doctors seldom diagnose a broken heart."

Stephanie nodded. "I bet that's how it would be for my parents, too. They're devoted to each other."

"Why aren't you seeing them for Christmas, Stephanie?"

She realized he must have caught the note of homesickness when she spoke of her parents.

"I couldn't afford to go back." She shrugged. "And they couldn't make it out this year."

"Couldn't or wouldn't?" He paused, his eyes questioning her. "They don't approve of this mingle arrangement, do they?"

"No," she answered unhappily. "They still believe when I live under the same roof with a man I should be married to him." She looked up in shock. "Lloyd, I didn't mean—"

"Calm down, Stephanie. I know you didn't mean. It's hard to ignore your parents' moral standards. That's one of the reasons I stayed married as long as I did." He walked toward her and removed the mass of icicles she still held in her hand. "Very seldom do we do things just because we want to do them. That's what makes tonight so special." He drew her into his arms, and she felt his heart thudding as she placed both palms against his chest. "We are only pleasuring ourselves." His words created boundaries, suggested all would be different when the sun warmed the waters of the ocean surging not far from their door, but she accepted that fact. A few hours of darkness remained, and she intended to use them all.

Rising on tiptoe, she curved her fingers around the beard-roughened ridge of his jaw and pulled him toward her, parting her lips as her tongue flicked out to follow the bow of his upper lip. As she sought to deepen the kiss, she was startled by a rumbling that sounded just above the belt of his trousers. She drew back, still cradling his face in her hands. "Are you hungry?"

"I didn't eat any supper," he admitted.

"Neither did I!" she exclaimed. "Can you beat

that? I don't think I've ever missed a meal and not realized it in my life! You cast some powerful spell, Lloyd Barclay!"

"Who needs food when you've got me?"

As if she had cued it, her own stomach growled fiercely, and she giggled. "I guess I do."

For a moment they stood silently, each wondering whether to offer the other something from their store of provisions.

"Would you like—" they began together, then broke off laughing.

Lloyd began again. "Let's do this equitably. You have some wine, right?" She nodded. "I have a can of shrimp I was saving for a special occasion." Stephanie smiled, remembering her remarks to Sigmund earlier in the evening. "I'll make shrimp curry," Lloyd continued, "if you can contribute the wine and some rice. Sound fair?"

"Would it unbalance the scales if I tossed a salad?" she offered, beginning to feel very hungry indeed.

"Not if you'll allow me to supply the dressing," he bargained.

"Agreed. Let's go. I'm starving." She pushed free of his encircling arms and moved with alacrity toward the kitchen, his laughter following her.

"Now I know the way to your heart! And they dare to accuse men of being motivated by their stomachs," he teased, opening the cupboard and reaching for the can of shrimp.

Stephanie poured them each a glass of wine to sip while they worked, enveloped by the steam from the boiling rice. Concentrating on their respective tasks, they fell into a companionable silence broken only by the gurgling water and the rasping of Lloyd's spoon against the bottom of the pan as he stirred the curry sauce. Stephanie congratulated herself on her choice of lettuce. The leaves held firm as if starched, tearing with a crisp crackle despite a two-day layover in the refrigerator.

"Anything you don't like in your salad?" she asked as she sliced fresh cauliflower, red radishes and plump tomatoes in with the greens.

"Yes. I hate mushrooms."

Stephanie hastily put down the mushroom she was cutting and picked out the pieces that had already fallen into the bowl. "Oh."

"You like mushrooms?"

"Yes. They're very good for you. When was the last time you ate one?"

He looked uncomfortable. "I don't know."

"Have you *ever* eaten one?" she accused, a smile tipping the corners of her kiss-reddened mouth.

"Certainly." He shifted his feet like a small boy. "And I didn't like it."

Carefully Stephanie chose the whitest, firmest mushroom from the green cardboard basket on the counter and held it under the running water, smoothing any dirt from the round cap with her thumb. "Just try this," she said, holding the dripping umbrella-shaped vegetable by the stem as she offered it to him.

He rewarded her with a pained expression, but

he lowered his head and his even white teeth nipped off a section of the cap. Straightening, he chewed it thoughtfully, then came back for a second bite, and a third, until at last he grabbed her hand and removed the last of the mushroom before nibbling hungrily on her fingers. "The mushroom was great, but this is really delicious," he murmured, raising his eyes to her face as he bent reverently over her hand, his tongue licking greedily over her fingertips.

"Your sauce will burn!" she laughed, jerking her tingling hand from his grasp. "Did you really hate mushrooms, or was that all for my benefit?"

"On my honor," he vowed. "Until this moment I really did hate mushrooms. You got any more? If not, I'll settle for fingers."

"Mushrooms will have to do for now," she said with a chuckle, "unless you want to forget about supper completely. I didn't realize fingers could be such an erotic zone." She washed another mushroom and handed it to him.

"I have a feeling there are miles and miles of uncharted territory to discover with you, Stephanie." The heat of his gaze threatened to melt her determination to finish the meal, and she turned back quickly to the salad bowl.

They ate at the counter, perched on Lloyd's bar stools. From the corner of her eye Stephanie watched Lloyd add a slice of mushroom to the prong of his fork. He ate the way he made love, with exuberance and appreciation. He also turned out a damned-good curry sauce, she admitted, biting into the firm pink shrimp as her tongue savored the creamy covering.

"This is really good, Lloyd."

His eyes smiled into hers. "Thanks. You whip up a mighty mean salad yourself."

"And what about the rice?" she prompted, testing his honesty. Rice had always been tricky for her.

"The wine's good, too," he evaded, a gleam in his tawny eyes.

"And the rice?" she persisted.

"The rice is mushy," he said.

"I know," she cut in quickly, sighing. "I always cook mushy rice."

"—just the way I like it," he finished as if she had not spoken.

"You do?"

"Sure. My mother taught me to like mushy rice. She couldn't cook it right, either." He grinned at her, and on impulse she leaned over, dropping a moist kiss on his scratchy cheek.

"Now that—" he paused and touched the spot with the tips of his fingers "—is what I call a 'like' kiss."

"A what?" she laughed.

"A 'like' kiss. Nothing to do with sex, nothing to do with passion, a lot to do with like. It's one of my favorite kisses." He dipped his head in her direction and she felt the warm, brief pressure of his lips on her cheekbone. "That's a 'like' kiss," he added unnecesasarily. "Now this—" he pushed their plates aside and reached across the counter to turn her toward him "—is not a 'like' kiss." As their lips met, hers flowered open under his gentle urging, and with soft drawing motions he pulled her tongue into the pliant recesses of his mouth. Her core of femininity throbbed to life as she heard him moan softly; then he pulled her gently from her perch to stand beside him on the floor. She felt the warmth as his hand slipped under her shirt and up her spine before he leaned away to study her upturned face.

"No bra, hmm? I like that, Stephanie." Deliberately he cupped the weight of one breast, his thumb brushing lazily across her taut nipple. Dizzy with passion, she laced her fingers behind his neck and watched desire darken his eyes as he continued his slow sensuous stroking of her breast. "Your place or mine?" His emotion-slurred voice quickened her already rapid heartbeat.

"Mine," she whispered. "I think I'd be seasick on yours."

The slow motion of his thumb stopped and he regarded her with surprise. "You've never tried a water bed?"

"No."

"Then you're in for a treat. Come on." He swept her up in his arms and started for his bedroom.

"Hey! I'm not sure I'm going to like this! Let's talk about it," she wailed, but he stopped her protests with a solidly delivered kiss.

"I ate your mushrooms; you can try my water bed," he announced with indisputable logic.

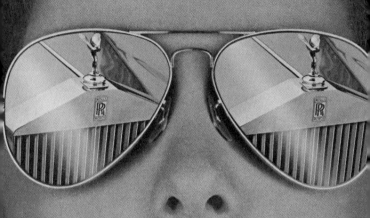

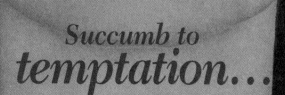

Succumb to *temptation…*

Could wealth, fame or power attract you to a man, even though you believe you love someone else?

These are just a few of the temptations you'll find facing the women in new *Harlequin Temptation* romance novels. Sensuous...contemporary...compelling...reflecting today's love relationships!

The passionate torment of a woman torn between two loves...the siren call of a career...the magnetic advances of an impetuous employer–nothing is left unexplored in this romantic new series from Harlequin. You'll thrill to a candid new frankness as men and women seek to form lasting relationships in the face of temptations that threaten true love. Begin with your FREE copy of *First Impressions*. Mail the reply card today!

First Impressions
by Maris Soule

He was involved with her best friend!

Tracy Dexter couldn't deny her attraction to her new boss. Mark Prescott looked more like a jet set playboy than a high school principal–and he acted like one, too. It wasn't right for Tracy to go out with him, not when her friend Rose had already staked a claim. It wasn't right, even though Mark's eyes were so persuasive, his kiss so probing and intense. Even though his hands scorched her body with a teasing, raging fire...and when he gently lowered her to the floor she couldn't find the words to say no.

A word of warning to our regular readers: While Harlequin books are always in good taste, you'll find more sensuous writing in new *Harlequin Temptation* than in other Harlequin romance series.

®™Trademarks of Harlequin Enterprises Ltd.

Get this romance novel FREE
as your introduction to new

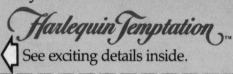

See exciting details inside.

"Some people claim a water bed increases a woman's response."

"They do?" He had reached the padded edge of the bed and held her for a moment longer.

"They do," he nodded solemnly.

"And does it?"

"We'll find out," he grinned, dropping her with a loud plop in the center of the undulating mattress.

"Lloyd!" she shrieked as the warm waves rocked her up and down. Desperately she rolled over, sending the mattress into new spasms, and grabbed for the padded vinyl at the edge of the bed. "How do I get off this thing?"

"Hang on; I'm coming in to save you," Lloyd replied, chuckling, tossing aside his shirt and stepping quickly out of his pants. He toppled next to her on the bed, and the rolling motion of the surface resumed as Stephanie clutched at him wildly for support.

"This is worse than a roller coaster!" she cried, listening to warm laughter bubble up from Lloyd's bare chest.

"Just hold still a minute, wiggle worm, and things will settle down—temporarily," he murmured into her curls. She followed his directions, aware of his fingers working at the buttons on her shirt. As he pushed aside the soft plaid material to nuzzle against her breasts with the moist pressure of his lips, she forgot about the movement of the bed as the now-familiar ache spread through her lower body. The mattress swayed gently as Lloyd removed her jeans and her delicate lace briefs, but Stephanie hardly noticed. She was beginning to enjoy the yielding quality of the bed that hollowed under her so perfectly, contouring to the curve of her hips, moving as she moved in response to Lloyd's questing mouth and hands.

Lazily opening her eyes, she found him watching her, his face mirroring the passion he roused in her.

"Touch me, Stephanie," he rasped hoarsely. "I want to feel your hands on me." She needed no more urging as her fingers traced a sensuous path down his spine. She stroked his firm buttocks before sliding across one lean hip to caress his manhood, drawing a groan of desire from his lips as she teased the sensitive tip. "Woman, I need you," he growled, rolling on top of her and parting her thighs.

She arched toward him, the mattress swelling under her in matching rhythm. His body fused weightlessly with hers as she sank deeper into the unresisting liquid. When the slow tender rocking began, she was surrounded by shifting warmth, yet anchored by the man she loved, who pushed urgently to the center of her being, demanding her body's answering release. Together they swirled in a vortex of sensation until both touched the center of the whirlpool in a blended cry of triumph. Later she heard the gentle cadence of Lloyd's voice. The words tangled together in her drowsy mind, and lulled by the soft sound, she slept.

MORNING LIGHT FILTERED THROUGH PALE LASHES, prying Stephanie from a dream she was loathe to relinquish. Lloyd was teaching her to scuba dive, and they swam in slow motion together through a technicolor world of brilliant coral and millions of darting iridescent fish. Sleepily she rolled over, away from the sunny glass doors. Her eyes flew open as the bed rolled with her. The water bed! Instantly she remembered, and just as quickly she realized she was alone on the quivering mattress. The total silence of the apartment told her Lloyd wasn't in the other room, either. Perhaps he had gone to buy a paper, or a batch of donuts, she thought hopefully, trying not to give in to the loneliness and depression that threatened to assail her. Awkwardly she climbed over the side of the bed and found her flannel shirt, discarded panties and jeans. Slipping them on, she padded into the living room.

The Christmas-tree lights had been unplugged, and the fireplace contained only ashes. Something on the tree caught her attention, and she walked over to pull a piece of paper from its branches.

"Stephanie," the hastily scrawled note began. No term of endearment, just "Stephanie." She read on, a growing sense of despair gnawing at her earlier happiness. "I've gone diving with Sharon. Back this afternoon. See you then, Lloyd."

7

SHARON? Who the hell was Sharon?

Stephanie searched her memory, but could not recall Lloyd mentioning someone named Sharon. Her early-morning dream threatened to become a nightmare as she pictured Lloyd experiencing the underwater world he loved with someone else, some person named Sharon. Stephanie imagined her easily. No doubt Sharon was tall and dark, a stunning creature in the revealing snugness of a wet suit. She could see Sharon's long hair streaming out behind her in the water, while Lloyd swam protectively by her side, both of them lost in the special privacy of their liquid domain.

Distractedly Stephanie wandered around the living room, memories of what she and Lloyd had shared there bombarding her, taunting her. She should have known, she scolded herself bitterly. He *had* stopped her from declaring her feelings for him. He *had* said, "No promises; no commitments." Now he was showing her exactly what he meant. He wanted to remain free for Sharon, or anyone else with whom he cared to spend time. He had no intention of tying himself to someone as he had with Jewel. Hugging her arms tight around

her, as if to squeeze the hurt away, she plodded into her bedroom.

"Those tawny eyes!" croaked Sigmund, jumping happily on his perch as she entered the room.

"Oh, Sigmund, how could you," she cried, giving way to tears.

"Pretty Stephanie," the bird squawked hopefully, cocking his head in confusion at his mistress's distress.

"You silly old bird," she choked, wiping her eyes with the tail of her flannel shirt. "You don't even know what you're saying, but sometimes you can have quite an effect on these crazy humans." She drew a shaky breath. "Come on. Let's get you out of that cage. I bet you're hungry." It was comforting to focus her attention on the brightly colored bird, and she took more time than usual cutting up bits of apple and a banana for his food dish. She allowed him to eat perched on the kitchen counter, something she would never have considered had Lloyd been there. After he finished, she gave him the roam of the apartment, carefully closing Lloyd's door first, averting her eyes from the rumpled bed.

Blaming her lack of hunger on the meal she had shared with Lloyd, Stephanie sipped a hastily brewed cup of coffee, enjoying the nurturing warmth of the ceramic mug between her chilled hands. She would clean, she decided abruptly. Cleaning was her standard diversion when deeply troubled, and her fingers itched for the scrub brush now. Only then did she realize the dishes from the night before were gone. Everything they had used had been washed and neatly replaced, almost as if Lloyd wanted to eliminate any reminder of what had happened between them. Well, two could play at that game, she vowed, rinsing out her cup. She would begin her cleaning with the fireplace.

She worked ceaselessly through the morning, the sleeves of her flannel shirt rolled up past her elbows and her shirttails tied snugly around her slim waist. By noon she sank wearily into the rocker, running work-roughened fingers through her curls.

"There," she declared to Sigmund with a tired sigh. Not a single particle of ash remained in the fireplace, and she had stacked the unused wood outside the back door. Let him make what he would of that message! All the Christmas-ornament wrappings and boxes were in the dumpster downstairs, along with the fireplace ashes, and every pine needle had been vacuumed from the floor with her small upright. Gloomily she stared at the unlit tree, which mocked her with its fragrance, reminding her of her willing surrender to Lloyd only hours before. At the moment he was with Sharon.

Giving in to the urge she had fought all morning, Stephanie pushed herself from the rocker and opened the sliding doors to the balcony. It was a glorious day, and the park overflowed with people making the most of it.

A young couple played Frisbee on the grass, the woman leaping agilely to capture the orange disk in her fingers. Joggers vied with walkers for space on the narrow sidewalk, and three surfers left their battered Jeep and scampered down the stone steps to the cove, fiberglass boards tucked under their arms.

Stephanie watched with a lump in her throat as two scuba divers emerged from the shallow water of the cove, removed their awkward flippers and trudged up the incline of the beach before easing off their air tanks. Although it looked like a man and a woman, she could not tell from where she stood if the man was Lloyd. But if it was, and the woman was Sharon, the woman confirmed Stephanie's worst fears as she dried her long dark hair in the sun and peeled the black wet suit from her lithe body.

Pain shot through Stephanie's chest as the man reached for the woman's hand, pulling her down next to him on the sand. Taking a deep breath, she battled the wave of nausea that swept over her. She turned her back on the scene, reentering the living room and closing the door with a determined thud.

"You know what I'm going to do, Sigmund?" she announced to the yellow-eyed bird clinging to the rocker. "I'm going to take the longest, hottest shower in history!"

Sigmund flapped to her shoulder and she decided to take him with her into the bedroom while she showered, just in case he considered becoming a tree ornament again. She cared not a fig about the tree, not anymore, but Sigmund might get hurt, especially among branches holding glass bulbs and decorations.

She closed her bedroom door firmly behind them and deposited Sigmund on top of his cage. Then, entering the bathroom, she removed her sooty jeans and shirt, and stepped out of her lacy underwear. Shoving her head under the drumming water, she doused her curls before reaching for the bottle of shampoo. Like the heroine in *South Pacific*, she wanted to wash her man out of her hair! Ferociously she worked to remove every trace of his presence, scrubbing his scent from the curve of her throat, cleaning every inch where he had touched her so intimately, so lovingly....

A sob escaped her lips as tears mingled with the steamy water cascading over her body. Damn it! Why did she have to love him? She wished she could be like him, willing to grab the moment, happy to move on to other things when the moment was over. Stephanie stood under the hot spray until her skin glowed pink and the tips of her fingers began to crinkle, but the torment inside her would not dissolve.

"Anybody home?" His cheery greeting froze her hand in the act of turning off the tap. He was back. "Stephanie?" He pounded on her bedroom door. "Can I come in?"

No, her soul screamed. *Not into my room, not into my life, not into my heart.* "Just a minute, Lloyd. Sigmund's loose in here." Her voice sounded reasonably normal, masked by the still-running water. She thought quickly. "He's been eyeing the tree again. Better not take any chances."

"Okay." She could almost see the broad shoulders shrug and turn away. "Have you had lunch?"

"No. I mean yes...I've had something," she called, desperate to avoid an invitation to share another meal. Did he expect to come back to her, after spending the morning with Sharon, and take up where he left off? The thought appalled her, and anger provided the strength necessary to face him. Dressing quickly in a clean pair of jeans and a yellow-and-white striped shirt, she ran her fingers through her damp curls before opening the door.

"Been cleaning up the place, I see," he observed, lounging against the kitchen counter, munching from a box of crackers he held in one hand. The sight of him there, smiling at her, nearly undid her resolve to put him in his place. His teeth flashed as white as the polo shirt stretched across his broad chest, and try as she might, she couldn't prevent her eyes from traveling over the form-fitting cut of his jeans, which emphasized...oh, God, she still wanted him. She leaned against the doorjamb, suddenly weak.

"Uh, yes, I thought it could use it," she mumbled. "Thanks for taking care of the kitchen before you...before you left." She had almost said "before you left to meet Sharon." But she wasn't quite that cool. She couldn't make herself say the name of her rival.

"You're welcome." His golden eyes slid possessively over her. "You look cute like that, all fresh and damp and curly, sort of like a marigold after the rain." He set the cracker box on the counter and took a step toward her. "I think I'll have you for lunch."

"No!" She backed toward her bedroom and he paused, a puzzled look on his face. "I mean, I...I have to feed Sigmund. He hasn't had anything since breakfast, and he really gets cranky when he's hungry, and I know how you hate to hear him screech, so...."

"What's the matter, Stephanie?" The question came softly, smothering her bright chatter like a goose-down comforter.

"Nothing," she babbled. "I just have to take care of Sigmund. He's a large bird, and he needs to eat three meals a day, and—"

"Are you upset because I went scuba diving this morning instead of staying here with you?"

"You have a right to do whatever you want with your time," she replied haughtily.

"That's right. And it disturbs me that what happened between us last night has apparently given you a feeling of propriety over me." His words cut into her like shards of broken glass. She was right. He wanted her in his bed when it was convenient, but he wanted total freedom to do anything else he chose with whomever he chose. Well, he could have that freedom, but he damned sure was not getting her back in his bed!

"I wouldn't dream of interfering in whatever you have going with...with Sharon!" she rasped.

"And you leave Sharon out of this!" His eyes

burned with angry fire. "She's a very fine lady, as I'm sure I mentioned."

"I don't recall you mentioning her at all," Stephanie replied, her voice cold.

He frowned. "I certainly did. Last night, as a matter of fact, after we...." He left a description of their passion unspoken, for which she was grateful. Vaguely she remembered something he had been saying to her the night before, but she had been so sleepy.... Apparently she had been mercifully spared a recitation about Sharon! "Sharon and I have worked together for years," Lloyd continued. "As I told you, we share the same lab space. She's practically my best friend."

"How marvelous. How could I forget someone you describe in such glowing terms?" she flung at him sarcastically. "How is it that you conveniently neglected to tell me about her until after you lured me into your bed?"

"Lured you? My dear young woman, you were just as much a part of the luring as I."

"And now I suppose you think I won't be able to resist a repeat performance," she interrupted, needing to hurt him. "Well, I'm afraid I wasn't that impressed, so you'll have to make do with Sharon."

"Sharon? What's she got to do with you and me?"

"If you can ask that, then we don't understand each other at all. I guess all you want is a shallow, uncomplicated roll in the hay, someone to warm your bed when it's convenient. You probably switch women as quickly as you change clothes." She wanted to wound him, inflict the same kind of pain she felt when she watched him reach out his hand to that tall beauty at the cove this morning.

"I don't think you have any room to talk," he countered, the muscles of his jaw working. "How do I know you don't have a date with Jeremy tonight? As far as I know, you're still 'practically engaged'—" he mimicked her tone "—to the guy."

"Come to think of it," she raged, "going out with Jeremy tonight is a good idea. A very good idea."

"Fine. As long as I can count on you being gone, I'll invite someone for dinner. I wouldn't want you to come waltzing through the door at an awkward moment, if you know what I mean."

She sucked in her breath. He would bring Sharon here? It had never occurred to her that his cruelty would extend so far. She clenched her teeth against the cry of anguish rising in her throat. "Don't worry," she whispered hoarsely. "I'll stay out very late."

"Then it's settled. I'm going to buy a couple of steaks and a bottle of wine." In an instant he was gone.

Now she had done it. She had committed herself to staying out half the night. She had no intention of calling Jeremy. He usually spent Christmas in the mountains and wouldn't be in town even if she wanted to see him, which she didn't.

Jeremy had been the first available way to get back at Lloyd, but the tables were turned when Lloyd grabbed the chance to have Sharon over for the evening. She wondered if he'd build her a fire—and if they'd lie before it, enjoying the cozy warmth of the lighted Christmas tree, the tree she and Lloyd had decorated so happily together. Would he then take her to his water bed? Would he...? She shoved her fists into her eyes as if to blot out the picture of Lloyd and Sharon together on the rolling bed, Sharon's dark hair streaming over the white smoothness of the sheets.

She had to get out of there, figure out somewhere to go for the night. Running to her bedroom, she flipped open the telephone book and thumbed through the motel listings. There. A budget-priced establishment far from ocean views and creamy stretches of beach. She couldn't take Sigmund, but some fresh fruit and a lettuce leaf should hold him until morning. Shakily she dialed the number of the motel and made a reservation for a single room.

"No, just for tonight," she told the clerk. She was trapped into this for one night, but from now on, she would be firm. Lloyd could take his dates someplace else. This was the last time she would be kicked out of her own home.

It was easily the longest night she had ever endured. Anticipating trouble sleeping, she fortified herself with lurid gossip magazines, a much-touted detective thriller and the latest television guide. Nothing worked. Lying propped against the laminated headboard of the single bed, she stared unseeingly at the wall-mounted black-and-white set, trying to concentrate on the frenzied hilarity of a sitcom. She glanced at her watch. Seven-thirty. Were they grilling the steaks, sipping wine as she and Lloyd had done while waiting for the meal to cook? Her stomach knotted as the images assaulted her.

With a heavy sigh, she slid off the bed and switched off the television. No use wasting electricity. A half-eaten turkey sandwich and a nearly full pint of milk sat accusingly on the bedside table, but she could not finish the makeshift meal. Her eyes scanned the tiny room, the dime-store prints on the walls, the tangled fringe of the flowered bedspread, the frayed cord of the lime-colored pull drapes. She had never felt so alone in her life.

Refusing to give in to the tears that pushed against her eyes, she sank back onto the narrow bed with the best-selling paperback thriller clutched in one hand, counting on the book's reputation as a cliff-hanger to get her through the night. But five pages into the book she laid it down, unable to concentrate.

"Damn you, Lloyd Barclay!" Flinging the book across the room, she dropped her face into her hands and began to sob—racking angry sounds absorbed impersonally by the acoustical tile over her head. After a long, long time, the sobs ceased, and she curled down on the bed, still fully clothed, to wait for the dawn. Sometime before the sunlight tried to work its way through the heavy drapes, she fell into a tortured sleep, her dreams filled with tall brunettes with long flowing hair.

The sound of doors opening and closing roused her, reminding her where she was as other guests prepared to leave. She rubbed aching eyes, listening to the cough of car exhausts and last-minute room checks.

"Have you got the small suitcase?" asked a masculine voice.

"Yes, but where's the room key?" queried a woman.

"I left it in the ashtray. Did you find the map?"

The voices died away, and she wondered if she was the only person left in the motel. She would soon remedy that, she decided. Enough of this stupid little room! After washing her face and brushing her teeth, she felt slightly better, but she longed for a change of clothes. Yesterday—years ago—it had seemed unnecessary to bring along a fresh outfit.

A glance in the mirror revealed a tousle-headed young woman wearing a rumpled yellow-and-white shirt. *I look like hell,* she admitted, reflecting that Little Orphan Annie didn't seem so appealing with dark circles under her eyes. Lloyd might well wonder what she had been up to the night before. *Well, let him wonder,* she thought bitterly, stuffing the sandwich, magazines and paperback into the wastebasket. Pouring the now-sour milk down the sink, she threw the empty carton on top of the magazines and gathered her belongings into the blue overnight case.

Chances were Lloyd wouldn't care anyway, as long as she kept out of his way so he could have his fling, she raged, grabbing her small case in one hand and her purse in the other. He better have enjoyed it, because that was the last time she intended to accommodate his exploits by finding somewhere else to go for the night! Next time he could work out other arrangements with Sharon, or anyone else who came along.

The aroma of grilled tenderloin still hung in the air as Stephanie pushed open the door. She peeked into the kitchen, wrinkling her nose at the plates in the sink, the broiler pan unwashed on the counter. *He must have been too preoccupied to do dishes this time*, she thought, revulsion churning in her stomach. She hurried toward her bedroom, anxious to check on Sigmund.

"And just where have you been all night?"

She whirled to find him leaning against the frame of his bedroom door, his rugged face unshaven, his white dress shirt looking as if he had slept in it. The lock of dark hair fell over his forehead, and the lines in his face made him look older than she ever remembered seeing him.

"I don't believe it's any of your business," she replied coolly, fighting the urge to walk closer, to comb the dark hair from his forehead with her fingers and kiss the grim lines from the corners of his mouth. He looked tired, as tired as she felt.

"You certainly gave no indication you'd be out all night, and from the looks of you, it was quite a night," he accused, his tawny gaze raking her disheveled appearance. "I considered calling the police, in case something had happened to you." Something—was it pain?—etched itself briefly in his face.

"Your concern is touching."

With an angry growl, he lurched forward, then stopped himself. "I have to protect my vested interest in this mingle," he said with rigid control. "If something happened to you, I'd have a hard time making that payment alone until a buyer came along for your half."

"I'll try to remember that. It's the best reason I can imagine for taking better care of myself." Sarcasm roughened her voice. "Now if you'll excuse me, I'll find out how Sigmund is doing."

"Not so fast." His low menacing tone sent a thrill of fear across her raw nerves. "Are you, or are you not going to tell me where you were all night?"

She faced him, challenging him with her eyes. He would not intimidate her. "I am not."

"Stephanie, so help me, I—" He made a quick movement toward her, and she jumped back, trembling.

"Don't you touch me, Lloyd Barclay," she choked. "Why should I have to account to you like some—some teenager?" Her voice rose a notch. "How would you like to describe your evening to me? How typical of a man! You think I should justify myself to you, but whatever you are involved in is nobody's business, because you can handle it, right? Well, I can handle my situation, too!" *I will not cry*, she vowed, biting down hard on the soft inner fold of her lower lip to stop it from quivering.

"That's not the impression I got the other afternoon," he said softly.

Was that concern she heard? She stared at him mutely, wanting to believe he cared, yet distrusting the tiny hope growing in her heart. "I...I was safe last night, Lloyd. I'm sorry if I worried you." Tears stemmed by indignant anger threatened to break through at this first sign of tenderness.

"You did. After Sharon left I—"

At the mention of the other woman's name, reality hit Stephanie with a hard slap. "And what time was that?" she interrupted, blinking the moisture from her eyes. "Three? Four? Five? How long have you been pacing the floor, twenty minutes?"

"Leave Sharon out of this!" he roared.

"*I* didn't bring her in," she rejoined sweetly. "*You* did."

"All right. I guess I did." She saw the anger drain from him, watched it replaced with weariness. "But the fact remains, in spite of all this women's lib crap, *Ms* Collier, that a woman out alone all night can be in great danger. Your safety was in question; mine wasn't."

"Was Sharon's safety in question?"

"No, damn it!"

"I'm so glad to hear it." She spun on her heel. "I think this conversation is over, and I'm going to check on Sigmund."

"He's fine."

She halted in midstride. "How do you know?"

From the corner of her eye she saw him shrug uncomfortably. "When you didn't come home, I wasn't sure what to expect. I've given him some fruit and changed his water. He...he was calling for you, and I thought he might be hungry."

"Th-thank you." She stumbled over the words,

thoroughly confused. He had not cleaned up the kitchen or himself after his reveling the night before, but he had taken care of her bird. It didn't make sense. "That's very nice of you, considering you don't care for Sigmund."

He eyed her strangely. "He's all right. I...um...I had him out in the living room for awhile, too." He gestured apologetically, and she noticed a bandage on one finger. "I hope you don't mind."

"No," she said, dazed. "He didn't bite you, did he?"

"Why would you think that?"

She indicated his hand. "You're wearing a bandage."

"Oh." He glanced down at his hand. "Burned myself on the broiler pan. Sharon insisted I put a bandage on it."

Zap. She clenched her hands at her sides. "Well, thanks for feeding Sigmund," she bit out. "I think I'll go take a shower."

"Stephanie. Wait a minute."

"What is it?" Her frayed emotions threatened to overwhelm her. She longed to retreat to the privacy of her room, to escape the haunting beauty of those golden eyes.

"Could...could we talk?" He ran nervous fingers through his dark hair.

She fought down the urge to refuse. Might as well have the whole thing over with now. "Of course." She sank into her rocker as he paced back and forth in front of the sliding door, feigning great interest in the pounding surf.

"Tomorrow's Christmas," he began, and she realized with a shock he was right. This was Christmas Eve. "Do you think we could declare a truce for tonight and tomorrow? It seems a shame to be at each other's throats like this, especially since—"

"Since what?" she broke in, irrational hope surging within her. Had he broken off with Sharon the night before? Foolish as she knew it to be, she dared to imagine a confession of love, the joyous scene as she ran to throw her arms around his neck. Her eyes lingered on his broad shoulders as he stood gazing out the window, his hands shoved in the pockets of his slacks, his shirt unbuttoned and hanging loose to reveal the dark hair curling across his chest. She could almost feel his warm skin against hers, the rasp of coarse hair against her breasts....

"I'm leaving on a four-week research trip day after tomorrow."

"What?" The unguarded exclamation signaled her shock, and she could have bitten her tongue. It was the last thing in the world she expected him to say, and grief welled in her like hot lava.

"Yes." He turned toward her, a masked expression on his unshaven face. "I think it's just what we need."

"I...I guess you're right," she managed to get out.

He nodded in agreement, his eyes returning to the expanse of ocean. "Scripps is sending a team down to Baja, California. It's been in the planning stages for several weeks, although I didn't see any reason to tell you before. But I thought you should know we only have to put up with each other for another day and a half before we get a four-week vacation. It might be easier for us to be civil to each other." He faced her with a taut smile. "Ready to hoist the white flag?"

She avoided his eyes, focusing instead on a point just behind his head. "Of course." Her own tight smile might crack if she chanced a quick look into the gentle eyes that had mesmerized her with love not long before. Four weeks. An eternity. He said it was a research expedition, and she had to ask, "Will...will...Sharon be going?"

"Yes."

Although she expected his affirmative answer, it hit her like a blow to her midsection.

As if she had opened a subject he wanted to discuss, he continued. "By the way, that brings up something else. I hadn't planned to discuss it until after the trip, but I guess the separation will give us each some time to think about it."

She tried not to imagine what he was leading up to, tried not to let him see her anguish. With a superhuman effort, she assumed an air of mild interest. "Think about what, Lloyd?"

"Renting my half of the mingle to Sharon."

8

"RENT? TO SHARON?" She must have misunderstood.

"Yes." His eyes swept the shoreline, as if searching for his next words there. "I'm afraid you were right all along, Stephanie. Once we became lovers—" his tongue seemed to have difficulty with the word "—the complications set in. I should have known you'd want a commitment from me."

"Have I asked for a commitment, Lloyd?" How dare he assume he knew her so well.

"Not in so many words. But you do. Subconsciously I guess I asked Sharon to go scuba diving the other morning to test your level of possessiveness. I came back to find you in a jealous fit."

"You arrogant, manipulating—" No words would come to adequately explain her indignation.

"Gun-shy is the word, Stephanie," he said softly. "I'm sorry, but you have marriage written all over you, just like Jewel did. That's not what I want right now. I'd hoped—"

"That I would be a pleasant diversion with no strings attached?" she finished bitterly.

"Was that so foolish? You seemed so hell-bent on that clinic, and I figured a divorced man with alimony payments would be the last thing you'd want. It doesn't make financial sense for you to get hooked up with me on a permanent basis."

"That made a tidy little package for you, didn't it? Almost like having an affair with a married woman."

"I just don't want strings on me, Stephanie." His voice was low, dangerous. "If I thought I could live in this place without wanting to touch you every five minutes, we could forget the other night ever happened. Maybe if I move out, we *can* forget it ever happened."

"Why not sell?"

"You know better than that. It could be months before I found a buyer. I can't last that long. Sharon's willing to rent, partially as a favor to me."

"I'll think it over." She needed desperately to buy a little time. Lloyd had found a solution for his peace of mind, but it hardly took care of hers. Life would hardly be easier living with Lloyd's girl-friend!

"You'll have a month to think it over...and so will I," Lloyd pointed out. "No decision has to be made today, or even tomorrow." He smiled at her, a touch of sadness in his face. "In the meantime, I promise not to foist my unwanted attentions on you."

She stared at him in silence. Unwanted? No, that was the problem. She wanted him too much. All the conclusions he drew about her—the jealousy, the marriage hopes, the possessiveness—were all true. Oh yes, she wanted his attentions, but she wanted more, and more she could not have.

"I think I'll take my shower now," she said,

dragging herself from the rocker, hoping her knees would support her.

"Good idea."

She left the room quickly, conscious of the rigid line of his back as he turned his eyes back to the ocean.

ALL DAY Stephanie fought the lethargy of her body, which reacted as if she *had* spent the past evening partying. The nagging pressure of a headache about to happen fulfilled its promise by nightfall, delivering ice-pick jabs of pain to her temples at regular intervals. She slept fitfully, stumbling to the bathroom in the middle of the night to swallow two more aspirin.

By morning she decided she would live, especially if she fortified herself immediately with a very hot cup of coffee. Holding that single thought firmly in her mind, she wrapped her terry robe around her and padded barefoot into the kitchen.

"Merry Christmas."

She blinked at Lloyd, regarding her over the top of his newspaper as he lounged within the shiny depths of the patent leather chair, fully dressed in shorts and polo shirt.

"Uh, same to you," she mumbled past a tongue still thick with sleep.

"Would you like some coffee?"

"Thanks, but I was just going to make—"

"Have some of mine. After all, it's Christmas morning."

"I...okay. Thank you." Her drowsy stupor began to evaporate before the warmth of his gaze. Instinctively she tightened the belt of her robe. "Have you been up long?"

"Yes." She felt his eyes on her as she reached to take a mug from her side of the kitchen cabinet. "I never could sleep in on Christmas morning."

A picture of past Christmases, the gay litter of wrapping paper, the hugs from her parents, the smell of turkey roasting, brought a rush of tears to Stephanie's eyes. Her blurred vision caused her to misjudge where she was pouring the coffee, and she splashed the scalding liquid on her hand. "Damn!" she wailed, jerking her hand to her mouth.

"What's wrong?" Lloyd was out of his seat in an instant and standing beside her.

"Nothing. I just can't pour coffee into a cup without getting it on me," she moaned, gingerly touching the reddened skin.

"I'll get some ice." He flung open the freezer door.

"You're going to fix me a drink?"

"It's for your burn," he said tersely, plopping several cubes out into the sink. "Let me have your hand."

"Like hell!" She jumped away from him, thrusting her stinging hand behind her back. "That sounds awful! I'm putting butter on it, just like I always do."

"Stephanie!" It was almost a shout. For a long moment they glared at each other before Lloyd's face softened. "Please, Stephanie, let me help. It hurts at first, but believe me, it's more effective first aid than butter. You'll see.''

Trust me, said his golden eyes, and mutely Stephanie held out her pink-stained hand. For reasons she could not explain, she had confidence in him. Perhaps it was his honesty with her the day before. At least he had practiced no deceptions. She knew where she stood.

Gently he cupped his fingers under hers. ''This will smart for a while, so grit your teeth.'' He bent his dark head over his task, rubbing the clear cube of ice in liquid circles.

Stephanie winced at the numbing cold combined with the sharp sting of the burn, but she did not pull away her hand. He was right; it hurt. Yet a comforting warmth settled over her at the sight of his bent head, the soft pressure of his hand, the intensity with which he ministered to her.

''That should be enough.'' He tossed the sliver of ice in the sink and raised his eyes to hers, continuing to cradle her hand in his strong fingers. Concern shadowed his bright eyes. ''How does that feel?''

''Terrible,'' she admitted with a grin. Reluctantly she withdrew her hand, breaking the intimate contact. ''But I'll suspend judgement until the results are in.''

''Always a wise procedure,'' he said, his eyes telling her he wasn't talking about burn treatments. Abruptly he straightened and smiled. ''Well! Enough of 'General Hospital.' It's Christmas morning, and I believe Santa paid us a visit last night.''

Stephanie's gaze flew to the Christmas tree, and she noticed for the first time that its lights glowed softly in the early-morning sunshine. Sure enough, two large boxes, one wrapped in red foil and the other in green, lay under it. "Oh, Lloyd...I didn't...I don't have...."

"You think I bought those presents? I swear a little round fellow who smelled like sweaty reindeer delivered them."

"Is that so," Stephanie giggled. "And I suppose he squeezed his plump little self down that ten-inch metal chimney, too?"

"Word of honor." Lloyd raised one palm in silent pledge. "Aren't you a little curious about what the old fellow brought you?"

"Insatiably!" She scurried to the twin packages and picked up the red one. Silently she read the tag tied to the candy-striped ribbon. *To Stephanie, in token of discoveries yet to be made.* She cast Lloyd a puzzled glance, then settled herself on the floor to open the package. It was fairly light, and her nose identified a faint but familiar scent, sort of like....

"Mushrooms!" she exclaimed aloud. "There must be two hundred mushrooms in here!"

"One hundred and ninety-nine. I ate one."

"Oh, Lloyd." She laughed up at him, her eyes bright above her freckled cheeks. "What a marvelous present. I can hardly wait to open the next one."

"It's not for you."

She stopped, her heart lurching painfully. It didn't take much imagination to figure out who it might be for. "I'm sorry. I shouldn't have assumed that—"

"It's for Sigmund." His golden eyes twinkled.

"Sigmund?" She stared at him blankly.

"You know the one, don't you? Kind of short, loud dresser, big mouth. Can't miss him in a crowd."

"You got Sigmund a Christmas present?"

"Not me. It was—"

"I know, I know," she said with a chuckle. "A fat little guy who smelled like sweaty reindeer."

"Absolutely right. Let me get Sigmund out of his cage and you can help him open his package." Lloyd disappeared into her bedroom and returned a moment later with Sigmund perched casually on his shoulder. Stephanie had a strange feeling it wasn't the first time the bird had sat there, either. Slowly Lloyd lowered himself, macaw and all, to the carpet beside her. "Okay, start opening," he commanded.

Her fingers flew over the taped flaps of the green package while Sigmund watched with apprehension, shifting his feet and bobbing his head nervously. "Sigmund doesn't like boxes," Stephanie explained as Lloyd tried to soothe the bird. "They look too much like tiny cages to him."

"Then you'd better get this one open fast, before he shreds my shirt," muttered Lloyd, grimacing as a curved talon hooked a thread on his shoulder.

With a flourish Stephanie opened the flap of the cardboard box. Her gasp mingled with Sigmund's

screech as she stared at package upon package of M
& M Peanuts.

"M & M *Pea*-nuts," squawked the large bird,
plummeting from Lloyd's shoulder directly into
the box, almost knocking Stephanie over in the
process.

"I think he likes his present," commented Stephanie dryly, easing the box of candy out of her lap.
Sigmund sat contentedly in the box, munching on
the colored treats that spilled from one ripped bag.

Lloyd snorted in amusement. "He looks like a
painted chicken sitting on a nest."

"If only he could lay M & M Peanuts, we'd be
rich," laughed Stephanie. She lifted merry blue
eyes to Lloyd's face, but her smile slowly faded as
she met the intensity of his gaze.

"Perhaps we already are, and we don't know it,"
he said evenly, and she felt the blood pulsing
through her veins like drumbeats.

"Lloyd, I . . . ." She stopped. She sensed his uncer-
tainty, knew her own. The walls were still up between them.

A sad smile tipped the corners of his mouth, as if
he, too, searched for answers and found none.
"Merry Christmas, Stephanie," he said softly.

"Merry Christmas to you, too," she returned. "I
feel bad that I didn't give you anything, though.
You've been so . . . so thoughtful." Her hand swept
across the two boxes.

"Ah, but you have given me . . . a great deal,"
Lloyd said slowly, his eyes seeming to memorize

her features. The silence between them trembled like fragile tissue paper.

I want to love you, Lloyd Barclay, but now it's impossible, her heart cried out. *And tomorrow you're leaving, and you'll be with her, not me. I want to lie with you once more before you go, sear myself into your brain, but I haven't the courage to ask.*

Resolutely she tore her eyes from his face. "I guess I'd better hide the rest of these packages of candy, before I have a sick bird on my hands."

"And I'd better start packing. There's a meeting of the research team tonight to check on last-minute details." He hauled himself to his feet, and she rose, taking care to wrap her robe around her as she got up.

"What time will you be leaving?"

"Early. Before you're up." His eyes searched her face, as if seeking the real questions behind the polite ones she was asking.

"Oh." She stood awkwardly, cursing her cowardice. "Well, have a good trip."

"Thank you. I'll be home four weeks from Saturday night, probably around suppertime."

"Is there . . . is there anything you need me to take care of while you're gone?"

His warm eyes melted into hers once more for an instant. "Just yourself." He turned and walked into his room.

STEPHANIE HOOKED THE FRONT CLASP of her underwire bra and surveyed the effect. The added support nudged the swell of her breasts higher, emphasiz-

ing her cleavage, and she hoped the garment was
not too suggestive. She did not want to overplay
her hand. Never having acted the role of seduc-
tress, she had no clear-cut idea of how to go about
the process. But one thing was certain: She would
try to change Lloyd's mind about their relationship.

She was not the same inexperienced young woman who had cowered miserably in her dorm room
after Gary announced that love and marriage were
outdated. She had not challenged him, had not
tried to keep him from leaving. Perhaps she hadn't
cared enough, she realized in a moment of insight.
With Lloyd, everything was different. Four weeks
of sleepless nights, of endless soul-searching, had
brought her to the conclusion that she must swallow her pride and try to win his love. She might
not get marriage—not after his experience with
Jewel—but he could learn to love again.

"You have given me a great deal," he had said
the day before he left. To those words she pinned
her hopes for a future with Lloyd Barclay, a future
that could begin on this day of homecoming.

Fresh from her shower and clad in lacy bikini
briefs and her new bra, she stood in front of the
open closet, pondering what to wear. She wanted
to strike the right note, something between indifference and outright provocation. In a few days she
might resort to a little number from Frederick's of
Hollywood, but for this evening she wanted a more
neutral outfit. She didn't want to frighten him.

As she fingered first one garment, then another,

she wished she knew what Sharon looked like. Many times in the past four weeks she had stood here, evaluating her own assets. Although she could never aspire to a tall, leggy look, she possessed good proportion for her size, she decided. Her breasts were high and of a decent size, and her bottom was round and firm without looking heavy. Her cap of golden curls softened what might otherwise be a too-strong jawline, and she trusted the deep blue of her wide-set eyes to distract Lloyd from the sprinkling of freckles across her nose. Besides, her freckles hardly showed up in candlelight.

Relatively satisfied with her physical appeal, Stephanie considered her strategic position. After all, she lived with Lloyd, at least for the time being. Sharon did not. Stephanie recognized Sharon's advantage during the past four weeks, but she doubted a research boat provided many opportunities for romantic encounters. At least she hoped not.

A sudden screech from Sigmund caused her to whirl in annoyance. "Listen, you, cut that out," she commanded, shaking her finger at the colorful bird, who blinked mischievous yellow eyes at her. "I think Lloyd is beginning to tolerate you, and I don't want to make a choice someday between you and him. After what I've been through with you these last four weeks, I might choose him in spite of our long acquaintance, you wild-looking feather duster."

If she had not known better, she would have sworn Sigmund missed Lloyd, too. Day by day he had grown more raucous and demanding, and he had seemed to be waiting for someone to come through the door. She doubted he had formed an attachment to the man in such a short time, but then, hadn't she? Watching Sigmund flap his wings noisily and scatter his seed around the bottom of the cage, she prayed he would settle down when Lloyd got back. Poor behavior on her bird's part would make her task more difficult.

Selecting an outfit at last, she unzipped a long-sleeved, pink velour jump suit and slipped it from its hanger. The color was reflected in her cheeks, she noted with satisfaction as she stood before the mirror. Maybe the added color would minimize the dark smudges that had become permanent features under her eyes during Lloyd's absence. The jump suit seemed a bit loose-fitting. Impatiently she fiddled with the zipper, adjusting it up and down before she finally settled on a point just above the clasp of her bra.

She chose a pair of wedge-heeled canvas slings for her feet, and decided against any jewelry except her small gold earrings. She must not alert him with the kind of elegant attire he found that night just before Christmas. Dabbing light cologne behind her earlobes, she wondered if taking down the Christmas tree two weeks before had been the turning point for her. Perhaps, she mused. She had put it off until the last possible moment, when the needles covered the carpet and the branches dragged nearly to the floor. Carefully she had stored the ornaments in a large cardboard box, and suddenly she knew she wanted to be the one taking them out again with Lloyd next year. She wanted to watch him flinging icicles on his side of the tree while she draped hers one by one on her side. She loved him, and somehow she would make him realize that she was right for him, that a commitment to love was not a prison sentence.

She consulted the clock on her bedside table as she fluffed her curls one last time. Sounding "just the right note" had taken more time than she expected. Her heart fluttered as she realized he would surely be home before dinner, and it was nearly that time. Should she cook something? She did not dare prepare a meal for two, which would look presumptuous. She discarded the idea of fixing something for herself. With nothing to do, she paced back and forth in the spotless living room.

In a flash of inspiration, she remembered the firewood stacked outside the door. Surely Lloyd wouldn't object to her using the wood to make a fire. Carefully she carried the logs in, holding them away from her to avoid snagging the jump suit.

Several sheets of crumpled newspaper later, she finally fanned a wavering flame from one of the smaller logs. She nurtured it, blowing gently on the tiny blaze as it licked tentatively toward the larger wood. Satisfied at last, she stood up, staring in dismay at her hands blackened by newsprint. As she started for the kitchen sink to wash them, she heard the click of a key, and then Lloyd was standing in the doorway.

9

"You're home," she choked out, welded to the spot by the sight of him, his broad-shouldered frame filling the small entryway, his scuffed suitcase in one hand and his corduroy coat slung over one arm. Something leaped in his golden eyes as he stood looking at her, something that made her heart jerk crazily in her chest.

"Yes," he said with a small sigh, depositing his suitcase on the floor and flinging his coat on top of it. He closed the door, and she thought how tired he looked, despite the caramel glow of a newly acquired tan. "How've you been?" His rich voice washed over her, just as she remembered it. His face was thinner, she decided as he raked the lock of dark hair from his forehead. He seemed to look at her so hungrily!

"Fine. I've been fine. How was your trip?" *How was Sharon? Have you missed me*?

He shrugged dismissively. "We accomplished some valuable research." His eyes broke off their scrutiny of her to sweep the kitchen and living room. "You've been cleaning, haven't you?"

"A little." She remembered her grimy hands.

"I...I used your wood to start a fire. I hope you don't mind."

"I believe that's what I bought it for." Some of the tension eased from his face as amusement twinkled in his eyes. "However, I'm not sure that's what you're accomplishing." He strode past her to the smoking pile of logs and she caught her breath as his fleeting nearness, the pine scent of his after-shave, filled her with longing.

He was right. The tiny flame she had nursed so patiently had died. So much for atmosphere, she sighed to herself, walking toward the pile of news-papers to try again.

"Want me to do it?" he offered, crouching next to her by the slate hearth.

"No, thanks. I've got a personal stake in this," she answered, smiling grimly. "I like to finish what I start."

"So do I," he said softly, and she knew without looking that he was watching her. She wasn't sure whether he was talking about her, or Sharon, or even his agreement with her to buy the mingle. Stephanie continued to stuff paper under the grate, refusing to meet his gaze, and she felt the slight movement of air as he got to his feet. "If you've got this under control, then I think I'll take a quick shower." He retrieved his coat and suitcase from the entryway. "Hot water for showers was a seldom-provided luxury on the research ship." He paused in the doorway of his bedroom. "How's Sigmund?"

"A little belligerent lately," she admitted.

"What happened? Did the supply of candy run out?" Lloyd smiled, and Stephanie couln't resist grinning back at him.

"As a matter of fact, yes. We're out of mushrooms, too."

"I guess we'll have to do something about that." He winked at her, then disappeared to take his shower.

Warmer and drier now, the wood responded more readily to Stephanie's efforts. Before long even the good-sized logs crackled merrily, providing the percussion section for Lloyd's cheerful whistle penetrating through the closed bedroom door. Replacing the fireplace screen, Stephanie rose and walked to the sink to scrub the newsprint stains from her hands. How right it felt to have Lloyd home, to hear him whistling in the shower as the fire blazed. If they were a normal couple, she would have begun supper, but she could not do that, she decided as she dried her hands and wandered over to her rocker, pulling it to face the fire.

"That makes a nice picture."

She had not heard him come out of his room, perhaps because of his bare feet. He stood facing her, silhouetted against the fading light from the sliding door, and she could barely make out his features, although she could tell he had changed to jeans and a knit shirt. He moved toward her, and the firelight glistened on the damp tendrils of hair that fell determinedly over his forehead.

"I see you succeeded with the fire." He hunkered

down next to her chair, and she had the insane urge to pull his head into her lap, to stroke the hair that clung damply to the nape of his neck.

"Yes, I finally managed it." Her throat constricted as she watched him stare into the flames. He looked so alone.

"Have you had dinner already?" He raised his eyes to hers.

"No. I wasn't feeling particularly hungry."

"Well, I have a big favor to ask." He shot her an apologetic smile. "I didn't leave much in my larder, so nothing would spoil while I was gone, and I came straight home instead of stopping at the grocery store."

Straight home. Her heart leaped with hope.

"Do you think you could lend me a few things until tomorrow?"

She gazed into his upturned face, knowing how much she had wanted to have a warm dinner waiting for him, yet so afraid she would overstep her bounds. "Sure." She tried to keep her voice light. "I'll go see what we have to choose from."

"Thanks, Stephanie." He stood to follow her into the kitchen. "I only have one request."

"What's that?"

"Let's not have fish."

"Why on earth not?" She grinned at him, and they chuckled together. It was a nice sound, she thought, and it had been so long since there had been any laughter in the mingle. Not since.... She forced herself to concentrate on the contents of the cupboard.

"You know what would really taste good? It's been years since I had it." He reached for a package of noodles on the second shelf. "Macaroni and cheese. Got any cheese?"

"I think so." She laughed and checked in the refrigerator. "Yep, I've got cheese. Is that really what you want?"

"Sure is. It's about as far removed from fish as I can think of. And this time I'll make the salad, with your ingredients, of course."

She nodded, not trusting herself to speak as he alluded so casually to their last supper together. That shared night of love had figured prominently in her dreams during the time he was gone. She wondered whether it had meant anything to him at all.

Silently she began her preparations for the simple casserole, clocking the oven knob to "bake" and taking a bag of whole-wheat rolls from the freezer. Lloyd worked quietly beside her, apparently absorbed in his own thoughts. Occasionally they brushed against each other in the small kitchen, but neither acknowledged the accidental touch, although Stephanie felt seared with fire at each point of contact.

At last they were seated as before, side by side on the bar stools, their thighs nearly touching, their fingers only inches apart. Stephanie wondered if she would be able to force a single bite past the nervous lump in her throat, but she found she was hungrier than she thought.

"What was your research about?" she asked,

buttering a roll and sinking her teeth into its warm softness.

"We collected several unusual specimens. That area is teeming with marine life, Stephanie. Corals, and sponges, and fish with colors you can hardly imagine!" After helping himself to another heaping spoonful of casserole, he turned to smile at her. "The macaroni's great."

"Thanks." She glowed with satisfaction at his praise of her simple meal.

"The nice part about most of that area in the Baja is the lack of human pollution. I get so sick of finding old tires and tin cans in San Diego Bay. The sea may provide lots of answers for the future, and we're in danger of lousing it all up...." He paused to butter another roll, casting her a sidelong grin in the process. "That's a little soapbox I get on, Stephanie. Sorry."

"That's okay. It's an understandable soapbox, considering your job."

"Do you have any soapboxes, madame psychologist?"

"A few, I guess."

"Like what?"

She hesitated, then plunged in. "Counseling agencies which lack the personnel to do a qualified job. People go in expecting to be helped, and they may come out worse than when they went in. Then they complain, and it gives the whole psychology profession a bad name."

"I wonder if some marriage counselors fit in that category?"

She winced. "Yes."

"I thought they might." He continued eating, as if the subject had no more interest to him, yet she doubted his nonchalance. Damn! She had not wanted to bring up that sort of subject.

"Was that the extent of your work down there, collecting specimens?" she asked, trying to regain safer ground.

"Pretty much. The most gratifying study we're doing though, is in its infancy. There's a marine animal which seems to survive well on polluted water, and may even be of help in cleaning up some of the messes we've made over the years."

"No kidding? What is it?"

"Sea worms," he announced proudly.

Stephanie's fork clattered to her plate and she wrinkled her nose at its contents. "And you wanted to eat macaroni?"

His infectious laughter drew her with him, and as they sat gasping for breath amid new giggles, she thought again how long it had been since she had laughed.

"I guess I didn't think of it that way," he managed to explain at last. "Sea worms are very big, and I just never made the association. Thanks to you, I just did." He pushed his plate away. "I think I'm full now," he said unnecessarily, grinning at her.

"Me, too. I'm sorry, Lloyd. You were enjoying that casserole so much. How about some coffee? I can't imagine that would have any mental images connected to it."

"Sounds good. We can drink it by the fire."

In a few moments they sat cross-legged in front of the leaping flames, each holding a mug of steaming coffee.

Lloyd took a slow sip of the hot liquid, then set the mug on the hearth with a deep sigh, leaning back on his outstretched arms to gaze at Stephanie. "It's good to be home," he said quietly. "I've missed you, Stephanie."

There, he'd said it. She set her own cup down with trembling fingers, trying to remain calm. "I've missed you, too, Lloyd," she replied honestly, not daring to look at him.

"May I kiss you hello?" His question came softly, hesitantly, yet his eyes smoldered with an emotion that turned her answer into a tiny gasp of surprise. The pressure of his lips was quick, a teasing warmth he withdrew before she could respond. He watched her with bright eyes, taunting, daring her to take the next step.

"May I kiss you hello?" she asked with a hint of a smile. He nodded gravely, and she saw the gleam of triumph before his eyes closed.

Challenged into the role of aggressor, Stephanie vowed the final triumph would be hers. Sliding one hand slowly under the green knit collar of his shirt, she drew him toward her, parting her lips and making darting forays against his mouth with the tip of her tongue. Encouraged by his sharp intake of breath, she slid her parted lips sensuously across his, her fingers tracing small patterns across the nape of his neck.

Suddenly his arms closed around her, pulling her roughly against his chest as his mouth ground down on hers in anguished need. Releasing her lips at last, he peppered her face with kisses as he choked out her name again and again, rocking her in his arms. Joyously she pressed against him, drinking in the passion that she hoped one day to turn into love.

"Stephanie, these weeks without you have been hell." His hoarse whisper warmed her ear. "I know what we said, but I—"

Stephanie silenced him with a swift motion of her hand, pressing her fingers against his lips. "Shh! You don't have to explain to me now."

She didn't want to explore their problems this evening. This was a time to show Lloyd how much she loved him, how good they were together. Then she might find the confidence and courage to discuss their future. The battle had begun, and Lloyd was in her arms. Hadn't someone said possession is nine-tenths of the law? Maybe it worked that way in love, too.

"But Stephanie, what about—"

Again she stopped him. Perhaps he wondered why she wanted this, why she was in his arms at all, but she did not want to answer those difficult questions now, not now. First she wanted to weave the magic spell only she and Lloyd could create. Slowly her fingers crept up under the front of his shirt, and amazed at her own boldness, she caressed the firm male nipples. "Did you leave the water-bed heater plugged in while you were gone?" she whispered, watching his eyes darken with passion as her nails scratched lightly across his chest.

"Would you like to test it and see?" His desire-roughened voice stoked the fire in her veins.

"Yes."

With a groan he swept her into his arms. In one lithe movement he was standing, cradling her effortlessly against him. "Are you sure?" His eyes searched her face.

"I'm sure," she answered with a radiant smile, and he squeezed her tightly to his chest as he carried her into the bedroom.

This time there was no long exquisite exploration of each other; their urgency was too great. Lloyd drew his green knit shirt quickly over his head before unzipping Stephanie's jump suit and pulling it deftly from her body. He paused only briefly to kiss the swell of her breasts before impatiently tugging the clasp of her bra free to gain complete access to the creamy mounds with their taut rosy peaks awaiting his caress.

"God, Stephanie, I feel almost like a rapist, but I want you so much," he rasped, wrenching off her lacy panties. She heard the delicate rip of nylon, but she didn't care. She wanted him just as desperately, and her fingers went to the snap of his jeans, then to the zipper. She could feel the bulge of his need under the denim, and she pushed the material away, her own body aching for him as his hands aroused her to a fever pitch. She heard his moan as her hand slipped beneath the waistband of his shorts, and then a muttered oath as he rolled from the bed and stripped off the encumbering garments. "Forgive me, but I can't wait, Stephanie," he whispered hoarsely. His face hovered over her as she opened her thighs to receive him, her face mirroring the passion she could see in his eyes.

"I don't need more time. I want you," she murmured, her voice husky in the darkening room. She watched his face as he thrust into her, watched his eyes close for a moment. When he opened them again, they shimmered as if with unshed tears. "Oh, Lloyd," she choked, her own eyes overflowing as he moved tenderly inside her. Gradually his motion took on a more insistent rhythm, and it was her turn to shut her eyes as remembered waves of pleasure carried her closer and closer to a familiar shore. At the moment of impact, her eyes flew open to see Lloyd's face, infused with happiness, watching the violent emotions he created in her. She cried out, clutching his strong back with her fingers, and felt him surge deeper as his own cry mingled with hers.

As he collapsed, shuddering, on top of her, Stephanie wrapped both arms tightly around him, marveling how easily she supported his weight on the water bed. Peace settled like a warm blanket around them, and Stephanie smiled into the darkness. It was going to be all right. How could she lose, when something as wonderful as this could happen between them? She was going to win his love. It just had to turn out that way. She felt his breathing even out, and knew he had fallen asleep.

He needed it, she thought, reaching to draw the covers over them. He had looked so tired when he got home this evening. As a languid feeling took over her body, she realized that she, too, was tired. And she knew, for the first time in four weeks, that she would be able to sleep all night long.

THE BED WAS EMPTY when she awoke, and for one terrible moment she feared he had left again, perhaps to be with Sharon. Relief flooded through her as she heard the clang of a frying pan against the stove burner, followed shortly by the aromatic sizzle of bacon. Probably her bacon, she smiled to herself, imagining his debating whether to wake her up to ask if he could use it or surprise her with breakfast. She liked his choice, she decided, stretching and rolling deliberately to set the warm mattress in motion. She enjoyed the fact that unlike her own bed, this one had no cold spots as she wriggled her bare toes across its surface.

"Are you having fun in there all by yourself?" Lloyd stood by the edge of the bed, spatula in hand, grinning at her antics. "I'd certainly hate to think I was being replaced by a water bed." He sat on the padded edge and reached to cup one breast under the smooth sheets.

"Not much danger of that," she said in a low voice, her cheeks suddenly hot at his easy familiarity with her body. Already his lazy touch was having a decided effect, causing her to squirm under his hand.

"Should you be tending to something on the

stove?'' she asked as a slight acrid smell wafted into the bedroom.

"Oh, yeah!" He leaped up with a chuckle. "Almost forgot what I came in here for." His chest heaved in suppressed laughter. "Do you like yours sunny-side up or over easy?"

She smiled mischievously up at him. "Sunny-side up."

"Me, too," he grinned.

"I hope you like your bacon well cooked," she teased, as he charged out the door to save the smoking strips from total disaster.

As soon as he was gone she eased her way out of bed, still not used to its undulating surface. Lloyd's bathrobe, black silk with red piping down the front, was draped casually over the end of the bed, almost as if he had left it for her. She grinned, remembering the first time she had encountered the robe, with Lloyd in it. Impulsively she slipped it on, the cool silk slithering deliciously over her skin, and tied the belt securely.

"I've heard your tirade about black, but you look sensational in that robe," Lloyd remarked, appreciation warm in his eyes as she walked into the living room.

She spread her arms wide, opening the winglike sleeves. "It's beautiful, Lloyd. Where did you get it?" Instantly she wished her question away.

"It was a gift," he replied shortly, and turned back to the stove.

Why didn't I keep my mouth shut? Sharon probably gave it to him, she told herself viciously. "I wouldn't want to get egg on it," she said quickly, "so I'll just change into mine before we eat."

Back in her own room, she noticed fresh water and bits of fruit in Sigmund's cage. Removing the offending bathrobe, she grabbed her own white terry from the closet before scurrying back to replace Lloyd's robe on his bed.

"Breakfast!" Lloyd called, just as she folded the luxurious silk over the end of the black bed. *Whoever gave it to him knew he loved basic black*, she thought morosely.

"Coming," she called back, trying to adopt a light tone. "Oh, how perfectly lovely." She stood transfixed, touched by his efforts. Although she had not heard him leave, he must have gone out early that morning, because the Sunday paper rested next to her plate. And one of their neighbors was minus two marigold blossoms, judging from the flowers springing jauntily from the neck of a wine bottle filled with water. Two wine goblets containing orange juice accompanied the plate of perfectly cooked eggs and slightly burned bacon, and a mug of coffee steamed nearby.

"Glad you like it," he beamed as his knife crunched diagonally through a platter of buttered toast. "Sorry about the bacon," he continued as he slid into the seat beside her. "It's difficult to be an award-winning chef when you have such tremendous distractions."

Stephanie followed the path of his eyes and realized the front of her robe gaped open just enough for him to get a clear view of her breasts. "Heaven forbid I should interfere with greatness," she laughed, recapturing a little of her earlier mood. She pulled the white terry more closely around her, retying the soft belt. "Is that better?"

"No, but I guess it will help me concentrate on my food." He sipped his orange juice, and she watched him as he drank, wishing she could taste the bittersweet juice on his lips, wanting to experience everything he did. "You going to read your paper?" he asked tentatively, setting down his glass.

She smiled. "Would you like to have some of it?"

His lopsided grin gave her an answer, and they began splitting up the sections, each of them surprised when they both reached for the gardening pages.

"And we don't even have a place to garden in," laughed Stephanie.

"I know. That's a drawback of this place. I'd like to have a yard one day," Lloyd admitted, and Stephanie allowed herself to dream of planting it with him, spending time together on their hands and knees, up to their elbows in the damp richness of peat moss, creating a garden.

Covertly she watched him devour an article about pruning shade trees, and thought with satisfaction that this was how a Sunday morning was supposed to begin. Lloyd was the picture of casual relaxation, clad in a clean white T-shirt and jeans, nylon running shoes on his feet, and the ever-present lock of dark hair falling across his forehead. Suddenly he looked up and caught her staring. "You reading the newspaper or me?" he teased, cutting into the soft yellow of his egg yolk with his fork.

"Oh, I can always read the paper," she responded. "You're more elusive reading material."

"Would you like to do something about that, Stephanie?" The question quivered between them, ambiguous and unanswerable. Was he asking because he wanted commitment from her, or because he was afraid of it? She could think of nothing to say as she looked deep into his golden eyes, unable to read his expression. She dropped her gaze and turned to the counter, picking up their empty plates.

"You cooked, so I'll clean up. I think that's fair," she said brightly.

"All right. And after that we'll go to the store and replace all your food I've eaten up." He seemed willing to let the subject drop, and she sighed inwardly with relief. Not yet. She didn't want the showdown yet.

"That's fine, but I'll need to take a shower before we go." She squirted the flowery-smelling dishwashing liquid in the sink and turned on the hot water, plunging the egg-covered plates into the bubbly mixture.

"Care to reconsider a certain water-saving measure I proposed a long time ago? My shower's big enough for two."

She wanted to ask him how he knew that, but she bit back the question. She could make love in the same bed Sharon may have used, so why be squeamish about the shower? "I might consider something like that," she replied, stacking the rinsed plates in the rack. "After the dishes are done."

"Oh, you might?" His voice came close to her ear as she felt strong arms reach from behind her, pulling her backward against the hard length of his body. "What can I do to convince you?" One hand slipped through the opening of her robe, while the other undid the tie of her belt. The garment fell open, exposing her completely to his roving hands.

"Lloyd! My hands are all wet, and I'm trying—"

"Very trying," he mumbled, nuzzling her neck as one hand found its way to the soft core of her being, and she gasped. "Here I am attempting to seduce you, and you're worried about the damn dishes. You're tough on a guy's ego, Stephanie." Relentlessly he stroked her as her knees began to weaken.

"Lloyd," she gasped again, gripping the edge of the sink for support.

"If you mention those dishes, I won't be responsible for my actions," he said hoarsely, pressing the hardness of his desire against her.

With a groan, she twisted in his arms, wrapping sudsy arms around his neck and pushing her hips hard against his, feeling the metal snap of his jeans bite into her skin. "What dishes?" she murmured before claiming his mouth and thrusting her tongue between the whiteness of his teeth.

"That's better." His voice was husky with passion as he wrenched his lips from hers and scooped her into his arms. "And now to the showers with you, Collier!"

Her toes curled on the cold smooth tile of his bathroom floor as she stood watching the glory of his body appear. Quickly he stripped off his T-shirt, pulled off his shoes and socks, and began to unzip his jeans.

"I do think there should be a cover charge for this show," he laughed, shucking the last of his clothes. "Ready?" He twisted the handles on the tiled wall of the shower stall, then turned just in time to see her drop her bathrobe to the floor. "Lordy, but you're a joy to look at, Stephanie Collier," he whispered. "Come here." He held out his hand, and when she took it, he pulled her gently into the warm spray of the shower. Under the rush of water he kissed her, pressing her slippery body against his, letting her feel his need as the water coursed over them, running in rivulets from his outstretched fingers pressed against the small of her back. "Ever tried it in the shower before?" he asked, turning her until she felt her spine pressed against the checkerboard pattern of the tile.

"Tried what?" She grinned.

"I'll take that for a negative answer," he growled playfully. "It's time for a new experience, my little marigold. Hold on to my shoulders, and when the time comes, wrap your legs around my waist."

He lifted her hips, and as she felt his pulsing warmth enter her, she locked her slender legs around him, urging him closer. But the decisions were all up to him this time as she clung to him, abandoning herself to the direction of his hands, to his soft whispered instructions as the water pelted them with its own form of liquid caress. Gently, gradually he built her response until the rush of water became a roaring in her ears.

"Now, Stephanie, now," she heard him groan just as the shock waves hit her heated body, and he stood trembling against her, gasping for breath.

10

"Okay, you can drive, if you let me buy a tank of gas." Lloyd added two more items to their grocery list.

"If you insist, but it won't take a tank of gas to go to the corner grocery store." Stephanie checked to make sure her keys rested in the bottom of her purse.

"I insist." The warmth from his golden eyes stirred embers of hope. She would win, she decided jubilantly.

Once inside the store, she chuckled, remembering her dream of several weeks ago.

"What's so funny?" Lloyd pushed a cart toward her, and when the wheels began to squeak, she broke into a broad grin.

"I had a dream about you once. You were chasing me down the aisles of a supermarket, and I couldn't get away because the wheel of my cart kept squeaking, letting you know where I was. When I woke up, the squeaking turned out to be some noisy sea gulls."

"Hmm. I vould say dat sounds like a neurosis, yah?" Lloyd stroked an imaginary beard and regarded her solemnly.

"Yah," Stephanie laughed. "You seem to know more of the jargon than I thought you would."

"I took a psychology course in college, as a matter of fact. Some of it was fascinating. Then I went through the marriage-counseling bit and got soured on the whole business, which really isn't a fair judgement on my part." Lloyd separated another cart from those jammed together near the door and joined Stephanie in wheeling down the first aisle.

"Unfortunately, that happens to many people," Stephanie commented, scanning the rows of canned soup for tomato.

"How did you happen to decide on psychology, Stephanie?"

She glanced over her shoulder, can of soup in hand, and discovered him leaning on the front handle of his cart, studying her intently. Disconcerted, she stumbled over her answer.

"I...I suppose there are several reasons, maybe some I'm not even aware of."

"Spoken like a true psychologist," he grinned. "But go on."

"For one thing, I'm an only child, and I had lots of time to myself to think about things. I spent most of that time wondering why people acted in certain ways. Psychology gave me some answers, and I found that quite exciting." She deposited the can of soup in her cart and consulted her list. "We'll pick up the frozen orange juice last, okay?"

"Okay." He pushed his cart beside hers, and she felt the light touch of his finger tracing the curve of her arm. "I think I could use some answers right now. Can you tell me why I'm running away from the most wonderful woman I've ever known?"

She met his gaze, astonished.

"Yes, I mean you, my little moppet. And you scare me to death. Why is that?"

"I'm sorry, Lloyd," she mumbled. "I certainly don't mean to—"

"Hey, it's not your fault. I just wondered, with all your training, if you can explain it."

He wasn't kidding. His topaz eyes impaled her with fierce intensity.

"You just escaped a very suffocating relationship," she said slowly. "Your fears are perfectly natural."

"And they're hurting you, aren't they?"

"Yes." She dropped her eyes.

"I'm sorry, Stephanie. I promised once I wouldn't do that." He shoved his cart forward impatiently, then stopped, rapping the handle thoughtfully with his knuckles. "Damn," he said softly, keeping his back to her. Suddenly he turned. "That's a beautiful waltz they're playing. Would you care to dance?"

Stephanie hadn't even heard the music until he mentioned it, but he was right. It was a waltz.

"Here?" she asked, peeking up and down the aisle at the growing number of customers and grocery carts.

"Why not?" He dared her with a wink. "Are you too inhibited?"

"If I were, I'd never admit it." *Besides, we need to*

hold each other right now, she thought, moving into his arms. For a fleeting moment she wondered if she even remembered how to waltz, but the graceful step came back to her in a flash as Lloyd maneuvered expertly around the shopping carts, whirling her past the dairy case and down the cookie aisle.

Stephanie reveled in the firm pressure of his palm against the small of her back, the brush of his thighs against her own. She forgot the other shoppers, the shelves of food, the glaring lights as he mesmerized her with magic eyes.

"Lloyd Barclay, I do think you're crazy," she breathed, oblivious to anything but the spell he wove with unspoken promises.

"Crazy about you," he said slowly, dropping a light kiss on her lips. As the music ended, he swirled her into a dramatic finish, bringing a burst of applause from those who had paused to watch.

Suddenly aware of her surroundings, Stephanie blushed bright red. "Lloyd, let's do our shopping now," she said in an undertone, barely moving her lips.

"If you insist," he said, smiling benignly at the crowd. "I think the fans would like an encore, myself. Isn't that a cha-cha coming up?"

"Lloyd, let's go," she hissed, tugging at his elbow until he gave in and ambled back to their shopping carts. But despite her embarrassment, she felt happy, happier than she ever remembered.

As they continued to shop, Lloyd carefully included all the items that were part of the previous night's supper.

"Not the butter, Lloyd," she protested, laying a restraining hand on his arm. "How much could you have used, after all?"

"That's not the point," he countered. "If it hadn't been for your generosity, I wouldn't have had anything much to eat at all, and I want to show my gratitude. So hush."

Their easy camaraderie lasted until the bags were stowed in the back of the Chevette, but Lloyd grew more quiet the closer they got to the apartment. When he made no attempt at conversation while they marked and put away the groceries, Stephanie knew something was wrong.

"I'm going diving with Sharon this afternoon," he said at last, and she understood. Fighting for time to compose herself, she focused on a gull just outside the glass doors. Crying plaintively, the silver-and-white bird arched like a Frisbee against the azure sky.

"Stephanie? Look, I made the arrangements yesterday. Do you want me to cancel them?"

Of course, you fool! But then I'll confirm your fears that I'll suffocate you. "No, that's silly, Lloyd. Go ahead."

"Would you like to go along? Sharon and I could teach you the fundamentals, and I bet someone at the institute has some equipment we could borrow." He continued to stack his food on his side of the shelf.

"No thanks." Her voice sounded strangled to her

own ears, but she prayed it had a degree of normalcy by the time it got to Lloyd. "I doubt if I'd be very good at it, anyway."

"Well... if you're sure...." He sounded genuinely disappointed. "The offer stands, any time you want to change your mind."

I won't change my mind, Lloyd. Not ever. I could never share you with someone else. "As... as a matter of fact," she chattered, needing to erase any ideas he had that she planned to stay home and sulk, "I think I'd better spend the afternoon catching up on some grading, anyway." She laughed, a tight nervous sound. "I might find it hard to concentrate if you were here."

"I know how that goes." He sounded unconvinced, and she wondered if he sensed her deep hurt. She might be able to keep up the fight, but chances were she'd end up crawling from the battlefield, her heart wounded beyond repair.

Lloyd closed the cupboard and walked around to face her, putting his big hands on her shoulders. "Sure you don't mind if I go?" He tilted her chin with one finger, and she forced herself to look at him.

"I'm sure," she said softly.

"Okay." He looked puzzled, and he bent and kissed her gently before releasing her. "Then I better get moving. We are supposed to meet at the cove in a few minutes."

Moments later, he stood by the door, his arms full of gear. "Oh, by the way, while you were getting dressed to go to the store I spent some time looking through the real-estate section of the paper. It's there on your rocker. I found several good possibilities for your clinic, and I circled them for you."

"Thank you," she mumbled automatically, her dazed mind still able to realize that was the correct response, although she felt like screaming. Like an obedient child, she picked up the folded newspaper and sat staring sightlessly at it.

"See you later, then." Lloyd fumbled with the door, juggling his equipment, but she sat woodenly, unable to rise and help him. At last he made it out the door, and she threw the paper across the room, wishing she had thrown it in his face before he left.

"Damn the man," she stormed, rising to pace restlessly into her bedroom.

"Such gorgeous legs," croaked Sigmund from his cage, his scarlet head tilted to one side as if he was indeed surveying her figure, clad in crisp white slacks and a navy pullover sweater.

"Sigmund!" She regarded him in exasperation. "There's only one person who could have taught you to say that, and he is not one of my favorite people right now, so please keep your comments to yourself."

"Study the ego. Study the ego," chortled Sigmund, hopping crazily from one perch to another.

"You'd like to get out, wouldn't you?" She opened the cage door and the large bird climbed out, using his curved beak and strong claws to reach the top of the cage. "Oh, Sigmund, what am I going to do?'' The yellow eyes focused on her, as if encouraging her to talk. "You can't understand a word I'm saying. Well, not much of it, anyway, but I wish you were as wise as you look. I could use some advice right now. How can I compete with Sharon? Just when I thought everything was going so well, he runs off to go scuba diving with her. How can I—'' She paused as an idea slowly formed. Lloyd had suggested she learn to scuba dive. She could not let Sharon teach her, but what about a stranger? What about professional lessons? Briefly she thought of the drain on her small savings account, the account that someday would finance her clinic, but she brushed the thought away. Sharon's ability to scuba dive posed a serious threat, one she could eliminate by learning the sport herself. She gazed out her sliding door to the cove. Somewhere, under its turquoise surface, Lloyd and Sharon were together. She had to enter that world, too, if she expected to capture Lloyd's heart.

THROUGH CAREFUL PLANNING, Stephanie managed to keep Lloyd at a distance for a few days. She scheduled her lessons in the evening, mumbling something to Lloyd about counseling sessions with clients. When she got home late each night, she had no trouble sounding tired, and Lloyd seemed to accept her lack of interest in lovemaking. She hoped her coolness would not drive him to Sharon, but she could not handle physical intimacy with Lloyd for the time being.

She was registered in a crash course, and one day

very soon she would surprise Lloyd with her new knowledge. Until that day came, she wanted to avoid his bed. Until her arsenal of weapons was ready, she decided against an outright attack on Sharon's position.

She spent an entire afternoon and a good portion of her meager savings in a diving shop, then stashed her new gear in the back of her Chevette. The week flew past, and with five nights of instruction behind her, Stephanie began to gain confidence in her underwater ability, although she had experienced nothing but the tank at the diving school.

No lessons were scheduled on the weekend, and she wondered how to deal with Lloyd for two days as she awoke to a sunny Saturday morning. She need not have worried, she thought bitterly, as he clanked through the door just before noon, his dripping gear under his arm. She was sure he had been with Sharon.

"Hi!" His broad grin registered pleasure at seeing her. "Giving yourself a break after a hard work week, I see." She laid down the book she had tried unsuccessfully to read all morning and looked at him, at the happiness radiating from his sunbronzed features. His jeans and T-shirt reminded her of the past Sunday morning, when they had— no, she would not think of that. After all, hadn't he just been with Sharon?

"Nothing like relaxing with a good book," she said, keeping her tone even. "Have a good time in the cove?" She hated herself for asking.

"Sure did. I wish you'd change your mind and try it with us sometime, Stephanie." His chiseled features took on a boyish eagerness. "Sharon is such a pro at it, and I'm sure she could teach you in no time. You'd really like her, and I'm anxious for you two to get to know each oth—"

"Well, I'm not!" She stood up abruptly, amazed that he would continue to suggest that she become buddies with this person with whom she was locked in combat! But of course he could not know that. He was so obtuse; he apparently thought she was happy with this little arrangement, in which she played one-half of his female-companionship team. "I'm not sure what kind of person you think I am, but I have absolutely no intention of letting Sharon teach me to scuba dive. I think it's wonderful that you're so casual about all this—" her voice began to quiver in spite of her efforts to control it "—but I'm just not that loose, I guess!"

"I've told you I'm not ready to be tied down again, Stephanie. I thought you understood."

"Intellectually, perhaps. But emotionally, I've got big problems when it comes to Sharon. Now, if you'll pardon me, Sigmund needs me." She turned away from him, but he caught her arm before she stepped out of his reach.

"So do I," he said, his voice low and menacing. "And I've been very patient all week with a woman who had no time for me. I've asked no questions about the fact you've been out every night, and I've accepted your statements about being tired. In fact, I knew you were. I could see it. So I told myself to wait until this weekend. I let you sleep in this morning because you looked as if you needed it. Then I come home, wanting what I've been missing all week, and you behave as if I were the lowest thing on earth. What's gotten into you, Stephanie? You knew about Sharon last Saturday night, but it didn't seem to make much difference then. Where's the warm passionate woman who melted into my arms last weekend?"

"So you admit it." She was livid with rage. "All you require of me is my presence in your bed. I satisfy some of your needs, and Sharon satisfies some, is that it? And you use us both, without making any commitments to either one. I used to think I hated Sharon, but I've changed my mind. I feel sorry for her." She spit the words at him, wanting to hurt him, watching in triumph as his golden eyes became those of a wounded animal. Then the pain was gone, hidden behind an impenetrable mask. He dropped her arm.

"All right, Stephanie." His voice chilled her with its cold impersonal tone. "I've kidded myself that you could give me some space, some time to work this out. I told myself your psychology training might even help. But we can't live this way, gouging at each other until there's nothing left. I'll talk to Sharon, see if she's ready to move in."

"And I'm supposed to accept that with no complaint? Maybe I don't want to live with your girlfriend, Lloyd."

"Do you have a better alternative?" he challenged quietly.

She did not. Maybe Sharon would be the lesser of two evils, after all. She had not been able to play the game, and she had lost. She wanted to get away, to submerge herself in total privacy. The world was no longer a friendly place.

"I guess I don't," she sighed, too beaten down to make any objection to Sharon as her new roommate. "Whatever you want to do." Slowly she walked into her bedroom and closed the door, hearing an answering slam of the outside door as Lloyd apparently left to enlist Sharon's cooperation.

All that money and time wasted, she mused, thinking of the equipment secreted away in the back of her car. The gear was to have been her key to a peaceful private world. Suddenly it seemed so inviting, to let the water close over her as she slid effortlessly through waving beds of kelp. She knew enough to make one simple dive, and she had all the necessary equipment. Tears blurred her eyes as she mourned the secret surprise she had planned for Lloyd. Angrily she brushed them away with the back of her hand and stood up. Today she would experience the underwater wonders of the cove, and Lloyd Barclay could go hang himself, for all she cared.

Quickly she changed to her red tank suit and threw on a terry cover-up. Pocketing her keys, she stomped from the apartment, stopping in the parking lot to get her gear from the back of the Chevette.

The cove was deserted, but she reasoned that

the divers were all underwater, taking advantage of the prime noonday diving time. Farther out in the cove, deeper than she planned to go, several temporary buoys bobbed in the waves. She remembered her instructor's suggestion that buoys help pinpoint a diver's location in case of problems, but she didn't need something that elaborate. She'd just go out a little way and come back, just enough to soothe her battered soul. Her air tank would last only about forty-five minutes, anyway.

She struggled into the tight rubber suit. Why was it such a chore this time? At the school it just slipped on.... Powder. She'd forgotten to sprinkle the inside of the suit with talcum powder. Damn. Several sweaty minutes later she stood encased in the pliant black outfit. Chilled ocean water sounded wonderful.

Impatiently she snapped on her safety vest and weight belt before easing on the air tank. Mask and flippers in hand, she walked to the edge of the waves, the soles of her feet leaving footprints in the cool, resilient sand.

Sliding her toes into the unwieldy flippers, she stepped backward, gasping as the first splash of icy water licked her ankles. For the first time she acknowledged the niggling little voice of conscience she had tried to suppress. She should not be diving alone. How many times had her instructor emphasized it, written it on the chalkboard? But alone was exactly what she wanted to be.

Her eyes moved to the dancing buoys. After all,

she wasn't really alone. This area was a thriving metropolis of divers, for crying out loud!

Wetting her mask, she adjusted it over her freckled nose, took the regulator in her mouth, and backed into the foaming eddies, stepping carefully over the rock-strewn bottom. The chilled water crept under her suit, sending shivers over her warm skin, but soon her body heat warmed the layer of water inside the suit and the cold bothered her less. Satisfied with the water's depth, she turned and jackknifed under the dark swells, peering expectantly through the glass of her face mask.

She almost forgot to breathe. So this was what it was all for—the hours spent in the practice pool at the diving center, the small fortune she had invested in equipment.

Before her lay a graceful kaleidoscope of color, nearly silent except for mysterious clicks and squeaks, noises created by the marine life that made a home in the cove. Slowly she began to swim toward the undulating golden ribbons of a bed of giant kelp. The freckled thirty-foot fronds beckoned her lazily, held aloft by gas-filled bladders the size of baseballs. Like shuttles of a loom, tiny fish wove in and out among the rubbery strands.

Stephanie couldn't see it all quickly enough, bewitched by the wealth of life surrounding her. She didn't know any of the names for things, except the kelp, but she would learn. There! That bright orange one, the one that looked like an oversized goldfish—she'd learn the name of that one first.

Otterlike, she propelled herself through the dense bed of kelp, trying to follow the gaily colored fish. A length of kelp brushed her leg and she kicked at it in irritation. The action swirled the water and another frond wrapped like the tail of a whip around her ankle. Sculling with one hand, Stephanie reached back with the other to free herself, but the rubbery frond seemed glued to her. Angry, she felt for the knife sheathed against her leg, but stopped before she finished the movement. The knife was not there. In her eagerness she had left it in the canvas tote on the beach.

All right, don't panic, she told herself, knowing fear would increase her consumption of air. She checked her pressure gauge, which indicated more than fifteen hundred pounds of pressure. Good. No need to worry until it dipped below five hundred. There was time.

Methodically she worked at the kelp with her fingers, but the tough membrane held her fast. A rock. Maybe a sharp one could cut through the kelp. In growing despair she scanned the immediate area, finding nothing within reach. Her eyes returned to the pressure gauge. Twelve hundred fifty pounds. *Still time, still time*, she told herself, afraid her breathing was becoming more rapid.

Okay, so I'm afraid. The internal admission helped. With greater calm she explored the tangled kelp with her fingers, trying to find an end she might unwind. But several precious minutes of tugging and probing yielded nothing. She clawed more frantically as Lloyd's words to Jeremy flashed through her brain. *Divers often take needless chances... chances... chances....* Good God, she could die down here!

Other people broke rules, she thought bitterly, and didn't get caught. How ironic that she, who lived by all the rules, should be shot down the first time she disregarded a warning. Five hundred pounds. The danger level. *Never dive alone.* She could see the words printed carefully in white chalk on the green board of the diving classroom. But she wasn't really alone, she recalled. There were other divers, the ones under the floating buoys. They should be coming in soon.

She tried not to look, but the bland face of the pressure gauge drew her eyes in morbid fascination. Three hundred pounds. Divers weren't supposed to walk out of the water with any less than two hundred pounds left. She peered through the murky water, straining for the sight of a human figure swimming toward her. She tried to focus, but a wave of dizziness made it difficult to see clearly. She shook her head, but the dizziness returned....

She snapped to sudden awareness as arms shoved her through the water. Her leg was free. Weakly she fluttered her feet, trying to help as someone guided her toward the slope of the shoreline. She turned her masked face toward her rescuer, but could not recognize the diver or the diver's companion swimming on the opposite side of her.

When they reached shallow water, the men supported her between them, and together they staggered up the beach to dry sand. As one helped

Stephanie out of her gear, the other shrugged off his tank and kicked away his flippers before sprinting up the concrete steps to the cliff above. Stephanie's eyes followed him as he opened a wooden box containing a red emergency phone.

"I don't think I need anything," she protested to the kind-faced man bending over her. "I'm just a little dizzy."

"We'll get the paramedics to check you out, just to make sure." He slipped out of his tank and flippers and crouched on the sand next to her. "I can see you're a beginner," he mumbled. "Supposed to put your weight belt on after your tank, not before. And didn't anyone ever warn you about diving alone?" His gentle concern brought tears of humiliation. If only she could plead ignorance!

"I'm afraid they did," she confessed honestly. "I...I guess I thought with all the divers out there...I didn't think I was *quite* alone." The excuse sounded stupid, and she knew it.

"Lady, that's a lot of cove out there! Do you know how easily we could have missed you when we swam back in?" His concern had changed to impatient anger, and she didn't blame him.

"I'm...I'm glad you didn't," she faltered.

"You should be. In another couple of minutes you would have been a goner. Did you know the reading on your pressure gauge?"

"Yes," she said meekly. She heard her rescuer mutter something under his breath, but the sound of the paramedic sirens drowned out his words. Sirens. That's all she needed to complete her total embarrassment. The high-pitched wail brought a predictable crowd of spectators, and Stephanie shut her eyes.

"Oh, my God." The familiar voice reached Stephanie above the murmur of the crowd, above the last dying cry of the rescue truck. Lloyd. She opened her eyes as he raced across the sand toward her, but it seemed to take forever for him to get there, as if the scene were being played in slow motion. She had time to see the grim slash of his mouth, the tightly clenched fists, the deep crease of his frown. And his eyes. Never had she seen anyone look like that. "Stephanie, what in hell?" He dropped beside her, panting, grabbing her by both arms, his contorted face inches from hers.

"Excuse us, mister." Two men in uniform shouldered Lloyd away from Stephanie. "This the one?" asked the shorter of the two, and the diver who had used the red emergency phone nodded.

"Really, I'm fine. I—" Stephanie pleaded with the paramedics, her eyes riveted to Lloyd's face.

"Just breathe from this for awhile, ma'am," instructed a voice, and she felt the rubber of the oxygen mask cover her nose and mouth as they efficiently lowered her to the sand.

With well-rehearsed movements the paramedics assessed her condition, but Stephanie was only vaguely aware of their efforts. The only reality for her burned in a pair of golden eyes that never wavered from the dramatic tableau on the beach.

The oxygen mask was removed and the paramedics asked her to stand and walk around. Satisfied with her stable condition, the men gathered their equipment and left. Gradually the crowd dispersed, and Stephanie thanked her two rescuers.

"Just don't go diving alone anymore, lady." said the man who had called the paramedics. The two trudged up the concrete steps and disappeared, and Stephanie turned to face Lloyd, sure he had overheard the last comment.

"You went down there *alone*?" His voice, hoarse with repressed fury, reached across the sand.

"Yes." She looked away, unable to meet his tortured gaze. "It was pretty dumb."

"What happened? Why did you have to be rescued?" His words scratched like sandpaper across her raw nerves.

"I got tangled in a bed of kelp."

"You what?" He blanched and sucked in his breath. "*You could have died.*" She realized with a shock that he was trembling. "Why did you do it?"

"I wanted . . . it doesn't matter anymore," she said with a sigh, bending to pick up her canvas tote from the sand.

"The hell it doesn't!" In two long strides he closed the gap between them, and his fingers bit into her upper arm as he swung her to face him, the tote banging against his legs. "I demand to know why you risked your life out there alone, with no experience, with equipment you don't know how to use, with—"

"That's not true!" she shouted, tired of being treated like a complete idiot. "I've been taking lessons. I know how to use the equipment. If I had remembered my knife, this never would have—"

"Lessons?" He dropped her arm abruptly. "What lessons?"

"Diving lessons. I've nearly finished the course."

"Why would you take lessons when I've offered to teach—"

"Maybe I didn't want to be your student!" she cried, backing away from him. "Maybe I don't want to have anything more to do with you, Lloyd Barclay!" Through a haze of tears, she stuffed her belongings in the tote and ran toward the steps, tiny explosions of sand marking her flight.

The telephone was ringing as she slammed into the apartment. Tossing her sandy bag in the bathroom sink, she jerked the receiver from its resting place, then swallowed in an effort to control her voice.

"Hello?" she said finally in an unsteady whisper.

"Stephanie?"

She frowned in confusion, not recognizing the well-modulated tone of the woman on the other end. "Yes, this is Stephanie."

"This is Sharon. Lloyd said I could come over tonight and meet you, if it's okay."

11

HATING HERSELF FOR EVEN CARING about her appearance, Stephanie stood before her bathroom mirror taking an inordinate amount of time with her face. Leaning closer to her reflection, she stroked the mascara wand over her light lashes, then backed away to evaluate the effect of the mascara together with the muted blue of the eyeshadow she seldom wore.

"I don't know, Sigmund. What do you think?" She turned to regard the large bird perched on the towel rack.

"M & M *Pea*-nuts," he squawked noisily.

"Is that all you care about? Don't you understand what I'm about to go through here, you dodo bird?" She sighed as she surveyed the freckled face in the mirror. "I wonder if you realize, Sigmund, how hard it is to look glamorous when a person has short curly hair and freckles."

"Pretty Stephanie," responded Sigmund loyally, and his owner favored him with a tiny smile and another piece of candy from the package on the vanity.

"You're prejudiced. But I appreciate the compliment, faithful friend." She stroked blusher across her cheekbones and applied lip gloss with her fingertip. "There. That is going to have to do." She walked into the bedroom to check the total effect in the full-length mirror on her closet door. The pale blue knit dress clung softly to the gentle curves of her small-boned figure, giving her an air of fragility tinged with subtle sensuality. A row of tiny pearl buttons began at the waist and ended at the demure high neck, which was fringed in delicate ivory lace. The same lace circled each cuff of the long close-fitting sleeves. A soft knit belt was knotted loosely around her waist, and the skirt fell in graceful unpressed pleats to just below her knees. She slipped her stocking feet into the gray suede pumps she saved for those times when she wanted to radiate elegance. This was one of those times, much as it hurt her to admit it.

The outfit hardly qualified as the average stay-at-home attire, but she planned to tell Sharon and Lloyd she was meeting someone later that evening, without giving them an exact time. That way, if she found it impossible to stay in the apartment with the two of them, she could beat a hasty retreat. She could decide where to go later.

"Stephanie?" Lloyd's voice sounded through the door. Again she felt the familiar surge of pleasure as his deep voice rolled through the syllables of her name. If only she could hate him.

"Yes?"

"Are you about ready? Sharon should be here any minute."

She strode the few steps to the door and opened it. "I'm ready."

His eyes widened appreciatively, and she felt her cheeks flush under his frankly admiring stare. "All this for Sharon?" he questioned softly, and she sensed the question he did not ask.

"Oh, no," she said airily. "I'm meeting someone later."

The light in his golden eyes faded. "Jeremy, no doubt," he said unhappily.

"I don't think that's any of your business."

She saw a brief flash of pain before his face became a stoic mask. "No, I guess it's not."

"Pretty Stephanie, pretty Stephanie," croaked Sigmund, flapping to the top of the cage.

"Smart bird," mumbled Lloyd. "Do you think you could put him in his cage, Stephanie? We don't know how he'll react to Sharon, and—"

"Of course." *If Sigmund understood the situation, he'd sink his beak into both of you,* she thought bitterly, retrieving the package of M & M Peanuts from the bathroom counter. Kneeling by the cage door, she spoke coaxingly to the large bird. "Come on, Sigmund. Time to get back into your cage. There's a piece of candy for you if you'll cooperate. Come on." The macaw cocked his head and looked at her as if she had gone out of her mind. "Come on, Sigmund. Don't play games."

"I don't think he wants to go." Lloyd closed the distance between them, crouching with her next to the cage. "Hey, Sigmund. This is for your own good, buddy. Just go in the cage, okay?"

"Those tawny eyes!" croaked Sigmund happily, enjoying the double dose of attention. Stephanie had never felt so close to throttling him. Her anger grew. It had been a harrowing day, and this show of independence by her pet was the last straw. She grabbed for him, intending to put him bodily in the cage, whether he liked it or not. With an indignant squawk, Sigmund flapped out of her reach onto the bed, then careened out into the living room.

"Oh, no," groaned Stephanie. "Now we'll play chase."

"Don't worry. I'll get him," assured Lloyd, taking the package of candy from her hand. She followed him into the living room, where Sigmund perched on the back of her rocker. "Come on, Sigmund. Have some candy," Lloyd crooned, but as he reached toward the bird, the treat extended between his fingers, Sigmund fluttered off the chair away from him. One wing caught Stephanie's reading lamp, sending it smashing to the floor.

"Damn it, bird!" Lloyd lunged after Sigmund, who flew squawking to the black leather chair. Stephanie rushed to capture him from the opposite side, and then they reached for Sigmund together, their grasping hands clutching only air as the macaw flew frantically toward the kitchen. Temporarily thrown off balance, Lloyd fell against the chair, knocking it over against the glass-topped table. With a loud pop, the clear top cracked neatly in half, just as Stephanie stumbled backward and sat down hard on the floor.

"Good grief!" Lloyd rose on all fours and evaluated the destruction with dazed eyes. "It looks like World War III." His shirttail hung out of the waistband of his slacks, and his hair was in careless disarray over his forehead as he shook his head in disbelief. Stephanie glanced around for the shoe she had lost as she tugged her twisted skirt back down to her knees.

"M & M *Pea*-nuts," croaked Sigmund nervously from the kitchen counter.

The corner of Lloyd's mouth twitched, and Stephanie thought she heard a muffled snort. All at once they were laughing uncontrollably.

"Oh, Lloyd, I'm sorry," Stephanie gasped, hoping she wasn't in the first stages of hysteria. "Your table—"

"Forget it. You were right anyway. It *is* ugly." He shook his head. "I'm still not sure how I got talked into buying that stuff. The salesman told me it was one-of-a-kind, and I think I know why. The guy who designed it was fired the next day. The chair's not even comfortable!"

"Oh, Lloyd." Her lopsided grin trembled at the corners as her tears of laughter threatened to turn to sobs. That damned chair. He could paint the entire apartment black, if only he'd stay. "Lloyd, we—"

The urgent peal of the doorbell sliced through her sentence, and she took a deep breath before scrambling to her feet. Mechanically she adjusted her dress and located her missing shoe.

"What is it, Stephanie?" He delayed answering the door. "What did you start to say?"

"Nothing. Don't keep her waiting out there, Lloyd," she said softly.

He held her eyes for one eloquent moment, then turned toward the entryway. "Make sure Sigmund doesn't fly out the door," he cautioned, tucking in his shirt.

"I will." Her heart pounding, Stephanie focused her attention on Sigmund, speaking to him soothingly, placing her body between the bird and the door. Behind her, she heard the melodious voice from the telephone call greet Lloyd warmly. The door closed, and Stephanie turned, bracing herself to face her rival.

"Stephanie, this is Sharon McNeil." Lloyd introduced them smoothly, as if they were meeting at a cocktail party. "Sharon, this is Stephanie Collier and the famous macaw, Sigmund Freud. Excuse the mess, but when Sigmund decided he didn't want to go into his cage tonight, we had the mistaken impression we could make him do it."

Stephanie mumbled something polite as she held out her hand automatically to the tall slender blonde standing uncomfortably before her. *She doesn't want to be here any more than I want her to be,* she saw with sudden clarity, and found herself warming to the tall woman with the timid smile. She was not the brunette on the beach—Stephanie had been wrong there—but it hardly mattered. She was young and attractive, and kept sneaking affectionate glances at Lloyd. All at once Stephanie knew what she had to do.

"Why don't we sit in the living room?" She felt

astoundingly calm. "We could all have a drink, and—" She paused, snapping her fingers as if remembering something. "Lloyd, I forgot to make a new try of ice, and we don't have much left. Would you consider running to 7 Eleven and picking up a small bag so we can have a drink? Sharon and I can get to know each other a little better while you're gone."

Lloyd straightened from his task of righting the black chair. "Are you sure there's not enough ice in there, Stephanie?" He sensed her subterfuge, she was sure.

"Just one or two cubes, Lloyd," she fibbed, counting on the fact he would not challenge her.

He shot her a questioning look, then shrugged. "I'll get my helmet and keys." At the door he paused. "I'll be right back," he said, concern in his golden eyes as he surveyed Stephanie and Sharon perched in the living room, face to face. "Will Sigmund be all right if I open the door?"

"Sure. He's calmed down quite a bit. Thanks, Lloyd."

"You're welcome." He shook his dark head in bewilderment as he slowly closed the door.

"You wanted to get rid of him." Sharon eyed her with curiosity. "Why?"

"Because I just figured out who the fly in the ointment is here, and it's not you, it's me."

"What in the world are you talking about?" The look in Sharon's gray eyes shifted from curious to confused.

"Wouldn't it make more sense if you rented my

half of the mingle, Sharon?'' Stephanie asked gently.

"Why should I do that?'' Sharon frowned, perplexed.

"Oh, come on, Sharon.'' Stephanie became slightly irritated. "I've known for quite a while that you and Lloyd have a thing going. He may have been momentarily distracted by having me around, but you're obviously better suited to him. You don't frighten him by asking for commitments, and I've decided after meeting you that I don't want to destroy whatever happiness Lloyd can find with you. He didn't want to buy this mingle in the first place, but I know he loves the view, and I hate to see him give it up just because we can't get along. So why don't you just rent from me? It would solve everything.''

"Not quite.''

"Why not?''

Sharon paused and folded her hands in front of her before looking Stephanie straight in the eye. "Because it's not me Lloyd wants. He's in love with you.'' Stephanie opened her mouth to protest, but Sharon waved her to silence. "I hadn't planned to say all this to you, but I think it's time someone stopped playing games. After Lloyd's divorce, we dated for about a year. I was head over heels—I won't deny it—but something didn't click with Lloyd. He finally told me it wasn't going to work. Fortunately, we've been able to remain friends. I still love him, I suppose, but a one-sided love affair isn't very satisfying, so I've started dating other people. I hope someday to find someone as terrific as Lloyd who will happen to think I'm terrific, too.''

Stephanie felt a rush of sympathy for this suddenly very fragile-looking woman in love with someone who didn't love her back. Her pain struck an answering chord in Stephanie's heart. "If that's the case," she ventured, "then what is going on with this renting business?"

"Lloyd's been attracted to you from the beginning, but he's had to battle his old suspicions about women every step of the way. I've never heard the whole story about his ex-wife, but I do know when a woman gets possessive, Lloyd gets nervous. I imagine he's been using me as a foil to keep you from getting too close."

"You're right."

Sharon nodded. "I thought so. When he became really frightened, he asked me to rent. But something happened today. He didn't say what it was when he called late this afternoon—just that he'd been walking the streets for a couple of hours, cursing himself for a fool. You were the most important thing in the world to him, he said, and you'd told him you didn't want anything more to do with him."

"That's true. I said that," Stephanie confirmed softly.

"Well, he wants to change your mind, but he figures the only way is to start over, without the tension of living together. Sort of an old-fashioned courtship is what he has in mind. By my living here, he can prove to you there is nothing between us, and I'm also supposed to find out how involved you are with this Jeremy fellow. He's worried about that a lot." She stopped speaking, but it took Stephanie several seconds to recover from the impact of her words and close her mouth, which hung open in astonishment through the recitation.

"You are supposed to spy on me?"

"I guess you could call it that."

"Why in heaven's name would you agree to all this, Sharon?"

She shrugged. "As I said, I care about the guy. Plus, I had seen the place, and the view is much better than I could ever afford. Lloyd offered me a very reasonable rent."

"Oh, Sharon, I'm sorry. After what you've told me, it would be impossible. And just for your information, I haven't been seeing Jeremy for some time. He's no longer in the picture."

"And how do you feel about Lloyd?"

Stephanie hesitated briefly, but found she could not lie to this woman with the honest gray eyes. "I'm afraid I love him, Sharon."

"Thank God for that." Sharon sighed. "I think you two can make it, but you'd better have a good long talk, maybe several long talks."

"About what?" Lloyd's overly cheerful voice cut into their conversation as he came through the door and dropped the bag of ice cubes with a noisy rattle into the sink.

"Everything," answered Sharon, standing up. "And I'm going to leave you two alone so you can get started talking to each other. Maybe Sigmund can teach you some things about communication." She chuckled when the bird responded to the sound of his name with a loud squawk.

"You're not leaving?" Panic seemed to grip Lloyd for a moment. "Aren't you staying for that drink?"

"Lloyd, we all know why you were sent to get ice cubes, and it had nothing to do with drinks. Stephanie and I had a chance to learn...several things...about each other. It's up to you, now. If you do it right, you may need that ice to chill a bottle of champagne." She left quickly.

As soon as the door closed, Stephanie leaped indignantly from her chair. "You were going to have her spy on me!" The sheepish look on his face melted her anger like sun on a snowbank. "The funny part is, it would have been wasted effort." She glanced at him shyly.

"Wasted?" The question was a cry of hope, and she hurried to put his fears to rest forever.

"Jeremy and I are finished. Have been for some time. We never were a very hot item in the first place, actually."

Concern clouded his brow. "Then if you weren't out with Jeremy all night just before Christmas, then who?"

She laughed. "Lots of people. A mystery writer, television personalities, gossip columnists—they all bored me to tears."

"I don't understand."

"I rented a budget motel room that night, Lloyd.

I stayed there by myself trying to read, watch television, even sleep, until I was sure I wouldn't run into Sharon when I came home."

"You crazy little moppet." His soft voice reached for her, even before his arms closed around her. "And I spent the evening chewing on steak I couldn't taste, imagining what you were doing with Jeremy. After Sharon left about nine, I paced the floor for the rest of the night, waiting for you to get home. If it hadn't been for Sigmund keeping me company, I might have gone stark raving mad."

"At least you had Sigmund." Stephanie glanced at the colorful bird, who had moved his perch back to the rocker, and looked nearly asleep. At the sound of his name his yellow eyes blinked open.

"Good morning, Stephanie," he croaked half-heartedly.

"Oh, Sigmund," sighed Lloyd. "I sure remember the first time I heard you say that. I was ready to cook you for Sunday dinner, buddy."

"And now?" Stephanie questioned, half afraid of his answer. Had he accepted Sigmund, especially after his performance tonight?

"I can't imagine life without that bird." His golden eyes smiled down at her. "Or without his curly-headed owner."

She searched his face, needing to reassure herself of his feelings. "Lloyd, I have been possessive about you, but I can't change that. I have to know there's no one else."

"There's no one else, Stephanie." His eyes looked directly into hers. "There never has been, really. I tried using Sharon as a protective barrier, but she's only a friend, nothing more."

"That's what she said."

"She did? That's what you talked about, too?" He shook his head. "You made good use of that trip to 7 Eleven."

"Everything just started pouring out after I offered to rent her my half of the mingle."

"You were willing to move out and let Sharon live here with me?"

Stephanie stirred inside the circle of his arms. "I thought that would make you happy, and suddenly that seemed the most important thing to do."

He threw back his head. "Oh, God, this thing came so close to being a disaster for everyone, especially this afternoon. I think I understand your motivation for taking diving lessons. You wanted to compete with Sharon, right?"

She nodded.

"But why did you take that terrible chance today?"

"Like most beginners, I didn't realize it was such a terrible chance. I wanted to be alone, and I figured I might never use my diving equipment after all, and...."

Lloyd shivered. "It's been so stupid, all of it. And to think you almost paid with your life. If anything had happened to you...." He left the sentence dangling as he rocked her in his arms. Suddenly he stopped, pulling away from her enough to gaze into her face. "In your revealing conversation with

Sharon, did she happen to say anything about my feelings for you?''

"Uh, she said something, I believe." Stephanie blushed as red as Sigmund's feathers.

"Good. But I want you to hear it from me. I love you, Stephanie Collier, and I want to marry you."

"You do?" She stared at him in wonder.

He laughed, a joyful sound. "That's not the proper response," he said, kissing her eyes closed. "You're supposed to say 'I love you, too, and I accept your proposal.'"

"Of course I love you, but—"

"Say that again," he demanded softly.

"I love you," she whispered, caressing his face with her eyes, "but—"

"No 'buts' are allowed after that statement." He bent his head to nibble one earlobe. "When can we get married?"

"Lloyd," she persisted, trying to maintain her train of thought as his tongue explored the inner curve of her ear. "You're still making payments to one wife. Are you sure you want a second one? We can live together, like before. You don't have to—"

Lloyd's mouth moved rapidly across her cheek to still her words with a short intense kiss. "Let me clear up a few things," he said, tilting her chin with one finger to look deeply into her eyes. "First, I understand Jewel is getting married again, so the payments should be ending. But even if they weren't, I still would want to marry you. When I realized what almost happened in the cove today, I knew you were everything to me. All this time I've been fighting a commitment which already existed."

"But we can be committed without a piece of paper, Lloyd."

"I want that precious piece of paper, Stephanie. It helps protect my vested interest."

"In the mingle?" she teased.

"In you, moppet," he growled, swooping down to plant a resounding kiss on her smiling lips. "Oh, Stephanie," he murmured against her cheek. "I want us to be married, to have children, to build our careers together. If we're lucky, I want us to be able to walk by the cove when our hair is gray and our kids are grown, and remember all the things we've shared since the first time we walked there. I want a lifetime, Stephanie. Can you give me that?"

She leaned back against his arms, wanting him to see the love in her eyes when she answered.

"Yes."

The word hung between them like a luminous pearl, and for a moment they both savored the sound of it. Slowly, surely, they closed the distance between them, their lips touching, sealing the promise they each made with the whole of their beings. Stephanie felt her body soften against Lloyd like molten wax as she pressed closer, glorying in the perfect way they fit together. She heard him moan softly against her mouth before pulling away to nuzzle her earlobe.

"Mmm, Stephanie, the material of your dress is so soft, I can feel your nipples right through it." He stilled. "Didn't you have to meet someone tonight?

Naturally I assumed it was Jeremy, but if not him, then...." She felt him tense, wondering if she had a liaison with yet another man.

She grinned, drawing away to bathe him in a look of love. "I'm not meeting anyone tonight, my darling. I had to have an excuse for dressing up to meet Sharon, and I wanted to prepare you for a sudden exit if I found the sight of you with Sharon impossible to bear." She watched his face relax into a smile.

"So you didn't wear that dress for another man, but for a woman. That's interesting. All those little buttons have been driving me crazy, wanting to undo them, wondering if someone else would have that privilege tonight." He ran a finger down the row of tiny fastenings, making her quiver with desire. "Dr. Collier, may I walk you home?" He slid his hand down her arm and linked his fingers in hers.

"Certainly, Dr. Barclay." Hand in hand, they strolled to her bedroom door, where she turned to face him. "Would you like to come in for a minute?"

"No." His eyes danced. "A minute will not take care of what I had in mind. That's an awfully long row of buttons."

"Well...." She considered the subject, then raised twinkling eyes to his. "Perhaps you could stay a little longer, then."

He bowed. "You are most kind."

Still holding his hand, she led him to the bed. "Do sit down, Dr. Barclay. Your feet must be tired after that long walk. Would you like me to take off your shoes?''

"Among other things.''

Releasing his hand, she knelt before him, easing off the brown loafers, then slipping her fingers under his slacks to peel one brown calf-length sock down over his heel and off his toes. After repeating the process with the other foot, she slowly massaged the soles of his feet, glancing up at him through darkened lashes. "Is that better, Dr. Barclay?''

Lacing his fingers behind his head, he laid back on the bed with a contented sigh. "Much better. If you can do that well on my feet, what wonders can I expect for the rest of me?''

"Would you like to find out?''

"Mmm.'' He wiggled his toes in affirmation.

Kicking off her own shoes, Stephanie moved to join Lloyd on the bed. Planting light kisses on his closed eyelids, she lowered her head to the expanse of chest her nimble fingers quickly uncovered, her tongue creating teasing circles through the fine mat of hair. Ever downward she moved, until she heard him groan with pleasure as she reached the taut muscles of his abdomen and her fingers worked with the fastening of his slacks. As she eased the zipper down, she felt the pulse of his desire just beneath her fingertips. Slipping her hands beneath the waistband of his shorts, she pushed away the remaining barrier of cloth, tugging both garments off just as his arm snaked around her waist, pulling her back to him.

"You're very good at that, ma'am," he said hoarsely, twisting his body to bring himself fully upon the bed. Shrugging out of his shirt, he began to inspect the tiny buttons on her dress. "But before you continue your excellent attentions to me, I have some business to attend to."

With maddening slowness he unfastened each smooth button, his lips following the trail blazed by his fingers, searing her skin. Her breasts throbbed in anticipation, and she arched toward him, trembling, until at last he reached the front clasp of her bra and flicked it open. She gasped as his seeking mouth found the hardened tip of her breast. Gently he tugged at the rosy firmness with his teeth as Stephanie tangled her fingers in the hair at the nape of his neck, urging him closer. "Oh, Stephanie," he murmured against the silken flesh. "It was worth everything we've been through to have this."

"Yes," she agreed, her voice a throaty whisper as his hands moved to her shoulders, pushing the pale blue knit from her body. Within seconds he removed her slip and panty hose and pulled her hard against him.

"This is what I've dreamed of, during those long nights without you," he crooned against her neck, his strong hands defining the curve of her hip. "Just to feel the whole length of you, your skin soft and warm against mine, waiting...." Gently his hand moved between her thighs, searching out the moist recesses of her need. "It's so good to know you want me, Stephanie."

She squirmed against the hand that built an aching response in her heated body. "Oh, Lloyd, I wonder if you know how much!"

"Show me," he rasped. With trembling hands, she explored his hard muscled body, caressing at last the velvet fullness of his manhood until he shuddered with desire, a desire that fueled her own passion. "Moppet, what you do to me," he moaned, rolling above her. He gazed with hungry eyes into her flushed face. "I can't wait any longer, Stephanie, love. I need you now."

"Don't...wait..." she gasped, pulling his hips toward her. As he plunged forward, she felt an explosion of joy she had never experienced. Together! They were completely, irrevocably together at last.

She awoke cuddled against Lloyd's firm body, which curled protectively around her under the antique quilt. "Lloyd?" She turned to face him, tracing the outline of his beard-stubbled jaw just visible in the moonlit room.

"Mmm?" His dark lashes fluttered, and his eyes opened a crack to peer down at her.

"Let's sell the mingle."

"Sell it? After all this?" Suddenly he was wide awake.

"I've just had the most marvelous idea." Her voice sparkled with eagerness. "If we bought a house, why couldn't I start my clinic in a part of it? Then I wouldn't need a partner to help pay rent, and I could have flexible office hours, and...." She looked anxiously at Lloyd. "Would you mind something like that?"

He smiled at her, his eyes golden with love. "I think it's a super idea, Stephanie. And with the sale and the prospect of Jewel getting married, we might be able to afford a place by the ocean."

"And a yard. Don't forget the yard," she bubbled, already mentally planting red geraniums and velvety petunias.

"And a yard," Lloyd agreed, lightly teasing the tip of her breast to arousal. "Although for the life of me I don't know when I'll have time to work in the yard, with all the distractions in the master bedroom. We'll only have one of those, by the way." He lowered his dark head to nibble gently at the taut peak, and Stephanie felt the slight bristle of his beard against her skin. The telltale ache began again, and she reached for him.

"And your water bed? Will we use that?" she murmured seductively.

"Kind of like it, do you?" he chuckled, his tongue flicking over her flushed skin. "But it matches that black chest. What about your calico?"

"Haven't you heard that eclectic decorating is in?" she said with a sigh, not really caring at this moment if his furniture had polka dots.

"No, but I think I want to postpone this discussion until later," he crooned into her ear, sliding a possessive hand along her hip.

"Me, too," she whispered, lost to any reality but his touch.

"Good morning, Lloyd," croaked a familiar voice.

Lloyd's head jerked up. "Sigmund?" he called into the darkness. "Is that you?"

"Good morning, Stephanie," continued the bird, his claws making little ringing sounds as he walked across the top of his cage.

"That's him," laughed Stephanie.

"That bird has incredible timing," muttered Lloyd, burrowing against Stephanie's breast. "I'll tell you another thing our house is going to have."

"What's that?" questioned Stephanie languidly, as Lloyd's hands elicited a predictable response.

"A separate bedroom for Sigmund."